KU-067-552

Amy Peppercorn
Beyond the Stars

J Brindley lives with his partner in the southeast of England. He is keen on music of all different types, and enjoys playing squash and generally training to keep fit.

John has two children, a girl and a boy, both of whom have been instrumental in the development of his early stories for young people. He likes to draw ideas and inspiration from all aspects of life, especially from the people he meets. That's what happened when he met Amy Peppercorn.

Why not contact Amy?
www.amypeppercorn.com

Also by J Brindley

Amy Peppercorn: Starry-eyed and Screaming
Amy Peppercorn: Living the Dream
Amy Peppercorn: Out of Control

Changing Emma

Amy Peppercorn
Beyond the Stars

J Brindley

Orion
Children's Books

First published in Great Britain in 2005
as a Dolphin paperback
Reissued 2006 by Orion Children's Books
a division of the Orion Publishing Group Ltd
Orion House
5 Upper St Martin's Lane
London WC2H 9EA

Copyright © John Brindley 2005

The right of John Brindley to be identified
as the author of this work has been asserted.

All rights reserved. No part of this publication
may be reproduced, stored in a retrieval system,
or transmitted, in any form or by any means,
electronic, mechanical, photocopying, recording
or otherwise, without the prior permission of
Orion Children's Books.

The Orion Publishing Group's policy is to use papers that
are natural, renewable and recyclable products and made
from wood grown in sustainable forests. The logging and
manufacturing processes are expected to conform to the
environmental regulations of the country of origin.

A catalogue record for this book is
available from the British Library

Printed in Great Britain by
Clays Ltd, St Ives plc

ISBN-13 978 1 84255 197 4
ISBN-10 1 84255 197 3

www.orionbooks.co.uk

This book comes with thanks to all those who entered the book title competition from the website. There were some really good entries, but not quite right for this book. Future books . . . maybe. Anyway, thanks.

Amy
XX

With special thanks to Swavek Zak for the quote.

*** One

What is it like to be a pop star? You probably imagine that it's all excitement and fun, with loads of money and stacks of other famous people all coming round and being famous and beautiful and rich. Well it isn't always like that. Nothing is. Not always: it can't be.

But then, sometimes, it is!

Sometimes that's just what it's like. Sometimes it's all excitement and fun and fame and feeling wonderful and great. On stage it's like that, when everything goes well. Like the open-air concert we did in the park, with my so-called archrival Courtney Schaeffer and my best friend Beccs Bradley. We were, I don't mind telling you, so good! I'd been doing a tour before that concert, performing in all the major cities and towns in Britain. But that concert, in memory of my good friend Geoff Fryer, that evening was special.

There were so many people there. Were you one of them? I spoke to you, didn't I? If you were there, I spoke to you, because I spoke to everyone that night. All the negative things about being who and what I am flew away from me as I flew without crying in memory of my dear, good friend. Every face looking up at me on that stage I knew, by sight. Believe it or not, I spoke to each and every face with every song we did, with every gesture I made. If you had been there, you'll believe me. There was no blood left pumping through my veins; I was pure, undiluted emotional adrenalin. But I was no different to anyone else there. That was the point. I felt like that, while feeling everyone else feeling like that. There was no audience. We were all in it together, every single last soul, every upturned face moving, every hand clapping, every foot leaping from the ground. The place was jumping, jumping. Amy Peppercorn pumping, pumping, pumping up the whole park into one wildly inflated stage upon which we all performed. There were no breaks, no talking or applause between songs. We just didn't stop.

Beccs was with me. She was with me absolutely, totally part of what was happening. The adrenalin running through me ran in my friend, just the same. We were together.

Courtney Schaeffer was there with us, but got lost somewhere in a little bubble of her own. At one point I could feel her with us, at another I could sense her floating away by herself, trying not to be a part of what Beccs and I were doing, what we were feeling.

We were feeling it. All over. We were brilliant, fantastic. It was like a new beginning. Yes, that's what it was: a new beginning.

After the concert the whole sound crew, the musicians, the dancers, Beccs and Courtney and I, all went to a club. Beccs and I weren't old enough to be there, but nobody was going to turn us away. The club owner, wearing a sparkly suit with his long grey hair tied back in a horse-sized ponytail, came out to welcome us. People were taking photographs. The DJ started to play a remixed version of *Proud* and the whole place was dancing to my music. Including me.

The only person not dancing was Courtney Schaeffer. As the evening had gone on, she'd become more remote, less obviously friendly to Beccs and me. We didn't mind; it was up to her.

We were having a great time. A great time! Even Lovely Leo was enjoying himself, now he'd accepted that he wasn't sending me home early to bed tonight. Not tonight. He had no authority over me: not there, not then, feeling like we did. Leo was dancing – and a very good dancer he was, too – along with the rest of us. Beccs was laughing. A very nice looking man kept coming over and dancing close to her, trying to talk to her. She was laughing. He was about forty!

I screamed. Nothing could stop me. My manager Ray Ray and Solar Records weren't a part of this, in any way. Even Lovely Leo was free, for the time being. We were all free, dancing in a club at the heart of a very special night of celebration. Geoff was by my side. Until I died, he'd never entirely leave me. Jag I'd already forgotten. Well, not quite, but at least I was trying. I had all my life yet to lead. I was young, just starting out. He wasn't going to stop me.

Courtney Schaeffer didn't dance at all. Beccs nudged me as Courtney positioned herself and posed and flirted with Beccs's forty-year-old. We laughed, Beccs and I. 'Both of her faces are so pretty,' Beccs shouted into my ear.

I didn't mind what Courtney said or did. Maybe she had said some of the things the press printed about me. Maybe she hadn't. Or maybe she'd said them all. All I cared about was proving to that type of newspaper and the celeb mags that I hadn't said anything back. Not intentionally, anyway. The papers had a way of making things seem how they wanted them to appear. They weren't lies, not outright lies, but it was hardly ever the full and unbiased truth.

Courtney looked over at me and smiled. It was a smile that creaked and cracked under the insincerity behind it. She had readily agreed to appear with me on stage in the concert for Geoff. But I'd asked her for one reason; she, quite clearly, had accepted for another entirely.

'Has she gone?' I asked Beccs later, when I didn't see Courtney anywhere.

'She slipped away when they all stopped taking any notice of her,' Beccs said.

'I'm still glad I asked her, though,' I said.

'You're the star,' Beccs said. 'It's you. She wanted to try to get a bit of what you've got.'

'She's all right,' I said.

Leo flapped over to us, insisting that we should be thinking about leaving. 'You've got to travel tomorrow,' he reminded me. 'And you've got school,' he turned and said to Beccs.

We laughed. Leo sounded like somebody's mum when he was like this, but he was right. Leo and I were off to France, and Beccs was going to school.

'What a contrast!' she said, in the back of the car on the way home. 'School for me, Paris for you.'

'But I envy you,' I said.

'You don't,' she said, smiling.

'I do,' I said, being quite honest.

'No you don't,' she said. 'You're Amy Peppercorn now.'

'I always was,' I said.

'No,' she said. 'You used to be just Amy Peppercorn. Now you're *Amy Peppercorn*!'

I knew what she meant. I hugged her. She was a much better friend to me than I was to her. I envied her, but she didn't envy me. She just liked me. She wanted me to be successful.

I wanted Beccs to do brilliantly at school, at university. She was like the other side of me, or what I could have been if I'd been as clever as she was.

'I like having a pop star as my best friend,' she said. 'Being on stage in front of all those people, it's dead right for you.'

'Not for you, though?'

She shook her head. 'Not for me. But you, you're alive like that, aren't you. You're really alive, I know you are. I can see it, feel it coming off you. Courtney Schaeffer doesn't have that, not like you do. That's why she'll never really like you very much.'

✲✲✲Two

'**L**ovely,' Leo said, 'my sweet, what can I tell you? The man's an ogre, you already know, but he's a successful ogre. He's a tyrant, a beast, but he gets what he wants, and that's more and more success.'

Leo and I were taking the fast train to Paris for a show, talking about my manager at Solar Records, Mr Raymond Raymond.

'You know,' Lovely Leo was saying, 'I remember you on that chat show, that Frank McThingy Show?'

'Frank Fisher.'

'Yes. I remember what you said on that show. Do you remember what you said?'

'I think so. Which part?'

'When you said about there being two different sorts of people in this world?'

'Yes. Those that make things happen, and those that have things happen to them.'

'Exactly that, Lovely. Exactly. That's Ray, the first type. He has to make things happen. If anything happens to him – *anything* – good or bad – he fights it like a mortal enemy.'

'That sounds mad.'

'Or infinitely sane,' Leo said. It wasn't usually possible to get Leo to be this serious. Lovely Leo sang and danced and played piano, mincing and mewing, trying never to let the harm of seriousness anywhere near. But now he sat opposite me on the express train through France, wearing a pair of his immaculate black slacks and a sparkly jumper, fiddling with an empty coffee cup as he spoke to me over the table separating us. 'There's no madness in him. I wish there were. Everything is pure reason and objectivity. Do you know what I mean, Sweet?'

'No, I don't.'

'Well,' he said, flicking back his hair, 'Raymond Raymond is sheer, naked ambition. Everything he does, says, everything Ray thinks is all geared towards getting him where and what he wants. We are all pawns in Ray Ray's life-size game of chess.'

Now I knew what Leo meant. Now I understood. Everything that Ray had done in getting Leo and the dancer Jagdish Mistri to try to control me, manipulating me through Jag's attention and Leo's care, was all to spread the Solar radiation of Raymond's recording company. 'That's why he hated what we did at the concert in the park,' I said, 'even though it was such a success.'

'Yes,' Leo sad, looking into the dregs of his coffee. 'Yes, that's why. You took it out of Ray's control. He can't accept that, no matter how successful it was.'

And it was. It was successful.

'Thanks for all your help in arranging everything for that, by the way,' I said.

Lovely Leo flapped his hand, as if swatting a fly. 'Oh, it was nothing. The least I could do – well, not the least – you were right, Ray deserved to have us all working against him, after the way he – anyway,' he flapped, with both hands flailing, 'anyway, Lovely, enough of all that. Let's talk about me. I'm far more interesting.'

'Yes,' I had to laugh, 'you are.' Leo was more interesting because he was fun. Ray was hard work and heartache. Ray, manipulating everyone, tired me out with his powerfully nasty influence; even as Jag Mistri and I had spent the night together, supposedly alone, he had pulled the strings that set us all dancing to his ear-achingly atonal tunes.

'And so are you, my Sweet,' Lovely Leo swatted. 'You've come through, you really have. I'm so glad. Lovely, you have shown more strength than Ray would have – let's just say he underestimated you. We all did.'

Yes, they had. They truly had. Now I felt strong, stronger than I ever had. Ray Ray, when he spoke to me now, when I allowed him to speak to me, used a moderated voice, carefully choosing his few, staccato words, almost politely addressing me from a distance, usually with my mother in between us. Both she and I were determined I would never be used and damaged in the future. Together, my mum and I were powerful enough to deal with that Solar tyrant.

'Please stay with me, Mum,' I had said. 'I need you with me.'

'How can I?' she said, touching me under the chin. 'What do I know about the music industry? I'm just a teacher –'

'I'll be much stronger with you there.'

'But I –'

'I can pay you, Mum.'

'That wasn't what I was going to say.'

'But I can.'

'I know you can.'

'Then, please – come to Paris with us?'

'I can't give up my job that quickly. I'll need to give them time to find a replacement.'

'Okay. After Paris, you're my real manager, not Ray. You can deal with him, Mum, can't you?'

She looked at me, long and hard. It wouldn't be easy for her to give up her job for me, I knew.

8

'Please?' I said. 'I know he'll still be my manager, really, but I do need you with me. You're the only person I know who can come anywhere near intimidating Ray Ray.'

So Leo and I were making the trip to Paris without my mum, which made me feel slightly nervous. However amusing and interesting Leo was, he was still a big part of the influence employed to use and to hurt me so much recently. Oh, I didn't doubt that Leo liked me and wanted the best for me. But his ears and eyes were Ray Ray's; so that despite what Leo might say to me, however much Leo's mouth assured me that he was on my side, I couldn't help feeling that everything I said to him, everything he saw me do got reported back. Leo's shadow in the Solar light cast a bigger, blacker outline than his own physical being, as if Ray were looming there above and round and beyond him as Leo fretted and flapped.

Lovely Leo loved Ray Ray, however much he tried not to. He couldn't help himself. Leo's advice to me came with the voice of experience, but with such a Solar glare about it, I doubted that I could ever now totally accept or trust what he said.

'Now,' Leo said, settling back, 'let's have a little chat, shall we?' As if we hadn't been chatting ever since we'd left London.

'Of course, Leo,' I smiled. 'What about?'

He glanced out of the window. 'It's your friend,' he said.

'My friend?'

'The new boy. Ben.'

'Ah,' I said. 'Ben.'

We were talking about Ben Lyons. My mum had suggested we helped Ben to get a job at Solar. Ray Ray had actually said once that he thought Ben needed proper employment, so all my mum and I did was to help Ray take his own suggestion to its logical conclusion. Because Ben did need a job. Released from the remand home in which he'd been placed following his part in the car crime that had led to Geoff Fryer's death, Ben's school and his schooling and his sense of purpose and worth had all come to a sudden end. He was in danger of getting himself into more trouble. And the last thing Ben needed was more trouble.

'Yes, Ben,' said Leo. Again he glanced outside.

'What's the problem? He's all right, isn't he? He seems quite happy to me.' Every time I'd seen Ben at Solar, he seemed to be doing fine; a little bit remote, or standoffish, but apart from that, and the smoking he'd started, he seemed okay.

'He's a runner,' Leo said.

I nodded. Ben seemed quite happy being a runner, smoking, hanging out in the studio with Big Ron, fiddling with the dials and switches on the sound equipment, laughing and jostling with the technicians. He had changed, of course, he was more serious than when I knew him at school, but seriousness wasn't always such a bad thing. I didn't care much for the cigarettes though.

Leo focused on me. 'A runner, Sweet. That means he's supposed to run around, helping out, running errands, not getting in the way, not hindering.'

'Hindering? Who's he getting in the way of?'

'Who isn't he?'

'But how is he getting in the way?'

'Lovely, it's just him. His attitude. I don't know what he – he has issues, obviously. But they shouldn't be brought into work. It's his mood swings. He goes from being one thing to completely another – he's unstable, Lovely. Somebody needs to –'

'But Big Ron's supposed to be looking after him, isn't he?'

'Yes.' Leo shook his head slowly. 'Big Ron's the studio manager. He – Ron's just Ron, if you follow my meaning, Lovely. He's – he's lovely, isn't he? But he doesn't manage anything. That old cliché, laid-back? That term was invented to describe Ron.'

'So what do you want me to do?'

'Sweet, if you don't try to have a word with him, I'll have to. One of these days he's going to upset the wrong person –'

'Ray, you mean.'

'Amongst others, yes. If he gets in the way at the wrong time!' And he shrugged. 'What can I say? Lovely, he's your friend. And that,' he said, 'is what I think he needs most of all – a friend. I know what happened with you and him and – you know. He needs some help.'

'Okay,' I sighed, 'leave it to me. I'll have a word with him, as soon as I can.'

'Thank you, Lovely. Thank you. Just don't leave it too long, will you?'

'No,' I said, looking at the outskirts of Paris slipping by outside. 'No, I won't.'

✱✱✱ Three

I sang:

I feel your beauty through and through
They don't know you like I do.
They don't know you like I do
They don't show through like you do
I'm so proud of you.
I'm proud of you.

The French audience applauded as if they'd seen and heard me before, as if they liked me. I smiled, enjoying myself in another country, very pleased to be there.

Leo and I had come to Paris so that I could appear on the Jacques Bonhomme Show, which was like the Frank Fisher Show I'd been on a couple of times in the UK, only without Frank Fisher to breathe dead cigarette fumes at me. I had been quite nervous, initially, about appearing on a French chat show, in case nobody spoke English. I knew that was unlikely, but I still wouldn't be able to understand them when they were talking to each other.

But Jacques Bonhomme came to introduce himself to me before the show and was so nice and so charming. He spoke perfect English, and was able to reassure me still further by telling me how I'd be given some little earphones to wear, through which I'd be able to hear translations of everything that was being said. Then he took me to my dressing room and made sure I had everything I needed. I didn't need anything. Jacques shook my hand.

A make-up artist came in shortly afterwards, and shook my hand. 'You are going to make my job easy,' she said, studying my face. She spoke with an American accent. She was looking into me so deeply, as if she were about to fashion a new face out of the material she was being given in mine.

'I am?' I said.

'Certainly. Good skin. It's easy. Look, what cheekbones. We'll bring those out a little more, to make you look taller.'

I laughed. 'Yes, please do my make-up so I'll look taller.'

'It's true,' she said, sitting me down, working on my face, telling me exactly what she was doing every step of the way. Nobody had ever taken quite so much trouble to explain before.

'Oh, yes!' she exclaimed, stepping back as I appeared from behind a screen wearing my startling red stage clothes. She'd done my hair too, and along with the green eye-shadow and the rest of the make-up, I did, in fact appear taller. And older.

'They'll love you,' the make-up artist said.

They seemed to, too, my first French audience. As I was singing *Proud*, I felt proud to be there, to be singing in France, especially as they'd all made me feel so very welcome. I felt special. Yes, special. Sometimes, back home, what with one thing and another, I'd lost touch with how special it was to be where I was, doing what I was doing; but it all came back to me there, on that little stage, feeling so good in the high red boots that helped to make my legs look so much longer than they actually were.

Jacques Bonhomme greeted me again with charm and genuine warmth after my song. 'Ladies and gentlemen,' he said, or seemed to say. I could hear Jacques speaking in French to his audience, but the interpreter in my earphones proved to be very good at voicing over him in English. He sat me next to his first guest, a man, a well-known actor.

'Ladies and gentlemen,' Jacques Bonhomme said, 'Amy Peppercorn is from England, where she is becoming a big star. Welcome, Amy.'

'Thank you.'

'May I say, you have a wonderful voice. Hasn't she, ladies and gentlemen?' A ripple of applause ran round the studio.

Jacques's previous guest, the actor, was still beside me on the settee. 'You are lucky,' he said, once the applause had subsided. 'You live in London?'

'Just outside,' I said.

'Ah,' he said, 'your London theatres. So wonderful. The best in the world. Do you intend to work in the theatre, with your voice?' he said. 'I'm thinking of *Les Miserables*. Have you seen it?'

'Yes,' I said, 'I have.'

'Still,' Jacques interrupted, 'there's plenty of time, isn't there, Amy? You are still very young. And it's a very good thing, to be so young, at your age, is it not?'

I laughed. The audience laughed with me. 'Yes,' I smiled, 'yes, it's a very good thing, to be young, while I'm still so young.'

'France!' Ray Ray had yapped at my dad. 'France first. Then after, the States. France, the States!'

My dad had turned to my mum. 'Did you hear that?' he said, as if she'd suddenly become extremely hard of hearing. 'France! America!'

'I heard,' my mum said. The twins, my little sisters Jo and George, were burying their faces in her armpits. I'd been teaching them to be wary of ghouls and horrid great ugly trolls. They hid their faces from Ray Ray whenever he appeared in the house.

'France! America!'

My mum nodded, impressively unimpressed. She was still a teacher, although she soon wouldn't be teaching. I had so much yet to learn from her. So did my dad, but barked, instead, like a smaller, redder version of Ray Ray himself.

'Amy?' my mum said.

All my decisions were to be my own. Ray had to understand this. My mother's tone of voice let him know where he stood, as he stood just outside the local lamplight of the wall lighting my dad had installed in our ever-changing living room.

'Amy? France? America?'

My dad had beamed, almost glowing with a pulsating red internal light. Ray stood a little to one side, sucking up the light. My dad might have been waiting for an answer from me, but Ray bristled, tense as a stick, furiously willing me to conform.

'Amy?' my mum said again, with the twins buried in her sides.

So I sat on a shiny settee in a Paris television studio watching French-speaking mouths moving, but hearing English words spoken. It was good, to be this young and to be a pop star. Jacques asked me how it felt to perform in front of thousands of people, live or on TV.

'It feels live,' I said. 'Alive, if you understand what I mean?'

15

'Like a theatre performance, rather than film work,' the actor said. 'Yes. It's as if you've really come alive, isn't it?'

'It's wonderful,' I said. 'I want to do it forever.'

'Then,' said Jacques, 'we hope you shall. Amy, thank you for coming on the show. Have you been to Paris before?'

'No, first time.'

'How do you like it?'

'I love it,' I said, because I did feel love for it, for the way Paris was treating me.

'Ladies and gentlemen,' Jacques said, 'Amy Peppercorn!'

The audience applauded once again. I stayed on the settee next to the actor as Jacques introduced his last guest: Adam Bede.

On came a gorgeous guy in a leather jacket and jeans, unshaven, with long black hair. Black eyes. He kissed everyone, absolutely everyone, running off into the audience to pick out some of the women in the front rows. They loved this. Everyone clapped.

Jacques had to go and retrieve him in the end, leading him back to the interview sofa. But Adam Bede wouldn't sit there. He shifted the actor along and sat next to me. 'Amy Peppercorn!' he said.

I smiled. Grinned, actually, as I saw on the video recording afterwards. Grinned and coloured slightly as he said my name again.

'Amy Peppercorn! I saw you, your performance in the park, in London.'

'You were there?' I blushed.

'Oh yes!' Adam enthused. 'You were fantastic! What a live performance! You are very special.'

The video of the show shows a glow in my cheeks red enough, at this stage, to light the faces of the three front rows of the studio audience.

'And,' he said, 'I know your song, the slow one? *If Ever*?'

'It's an old song, actually,' I managed to say.

'Not in France it isn't,' he said. 'We don't know it. But when you sing it – oh! Shall we sing together? Shall we?'

The audience clapped their appreciation. Jacques indicated the small stage with a flourish of his palm.

'Not the sad song,' I said, as he led me to the stage.

'No?' he said. 'No. I know your other song, the one you did. *Proud*? We'll do it again, shall we, but together, eh? Shall we do it together? I know your songs.'

On the way back on the train, I called Beccs. The show had been such a surprising success, I wanted to tell her all about it and to ask if she minded if Ben came out with us the next night. We'd arranged to go for dinner somewhere good, before I had to go off to America. I wanted Ben to come with us, to see if I could get a chance to have a quiet word with him, as I'd promised Leo.

'I don't mind if Ben comes,' Beccs said. 'Why should I mind? It's good. But tell me about the show. Tell me all about Paris.'

Adam and I had sung *Proud*. He definitely did know my songs. I'd never heard of him, but he seemed to know all about me.

'*If Ever*,' he'd said, when we sat down again, having sung *Proud* together, 'it is a beautiful song. Very beautiful.'

He held an open-palmed hand out to me. I took his hand. The audience clapped.

'You know Amy very well,' Jacques Bonhomme said.

'No,' Adam said, 'not yet.'

He looked at me. He had beautiful dark eyes. But, I had to

admit, I couldn't help but see in them, through the reflection of Jag Mistri, the shallow, single-minded ambition of Solar Records and all their equivalents. Adam smiled at me. I had to recognise the smile.

'Oh,' Jacques also smiled, 'very good!'

'Yes,' said Adam. 'I have a song,' he said, to me. 'I have a song I think you will like. I'd like to give it to you.'

'Give it to me?'

'Yes. It is called *Never Let You Go*. I will translate it for you. It is very beautiful, too.'

'Then,' Jacques said, 'you will come back, Amy, soon, to sing *Never Let You Go*, for us? Yes?'

The audience applauded. Adam Bede was giving me a song, one written by him and his songwriting partner.

'Yes, please,' I said.

'He's giving you his song?' Beccs said on my new mobile as Leo and I hurried on the fast train so smoothly back through France.

'Yes,' I said, glancing at Leo as he sat glancing over at me. I was further up the carriage, heading back from the loo, stopping to call Beccs. 'A song he's written. He thinks it's beautiful.'

'What do you think?'

'I don't know. I haven't heard it yet.'

'But the show was good?'

'Yes. In the end, very good. I was really nervous about doing a chat show in France at first. After being on the stupid Frank Fisher Show, all I could think was I didn't want to do any more stupid chat shows, ever again – hang on a minute.' Leo was coming by, making his way up the carriage towards the toilet. I had to move over to let him go by. 'Are you still there?' I said to Beccs.

She was still there. Beccs was always there. She was my contact with the other life, the one I might have led if I'd been better at studying than singing. My mum couldn't do this for me; she was my mum, whatever my life was. 'I'm still here,' Beccs said.

'In the end,' I said, 'the show was really good. Fantastic, in fact. Anyway – tell me what's happening at school,' I said. I always asked her to tell me. It was like hearing a story from my lost childhood.

But she said, 'You haven't finished telling me about the show yet. And Adam Bede!'

'He's a big star in France.'

'And good looking?'

'No. Fantastic looking. But I'm not –'

'Oh, really?'

'I'm not. Really. We sang *Proud* together. It was good. Something might come of it. But I'm not interested in him, or anyone. Really.'

✳✳✳Four

France was so different from England, for me. In Paris, nobody knew who I was. In London, people recognised me. 'Keep walking,' Leo would say to me. People hardly ever tried to stop me if I carried on as if nothing was happening. There'd be a puzzled look for a few moments as we approached, as if to say, 'I know I know you, but I can't remember from where.' Then the penny dropped. There'd be a look then, as a decision was made whether to speak or not. 'Keep walking,' Leo would always say.

But I didn't always want to walk by. I still liked it whenever people recognised me. It made me feel so special. As if I could do anything, achieve anything. Some stars made me sick the way they went on about how much they hated being in the public eye all the time. That attitude always struck me as hypocritical and silly. It was nice to walk about in Paris like any other British tourist; but it was much nicer to be the centre of attention at Waterloo station in London.

As soon as we had to stop to get through a ticket barrier, an old lady said to me, 'You're Amy Peppercorn, aren't you?'

I smiled. A gentle old lady had taken the trouble to ask me that.

'Ooh,' she said, 'I've loved that song, *If Ever*, nearly all my life. But I've never heard it done like you did it. You made me cry, young lady. I hadn't cried for years, but you made me cry.'

I'd done with crying, myself. But I felt like hugging her. And I did.

'Can I have your autograph,' she said, 'for my grandson? Oh, and one for my daughter's stepdaughter. And one for . . . '

Leo was hopping from one foot to the other as if he needed to go to the loo again. We had some kind of photo-shoot to get to, for a magazine; I couldn't remember the details. A small crowd had gathered, most with pieces of paper, books, and even one with a photograph of me to sign. 'It was in the magazine I was reading,' the woman said. 'My son will be so excited.'

'Don't let me come out without signed photos next time,' I said to Leo.

'Lovely,' he said, 'you simply don't have the time to stop for every single –'

I turned my back on him. I still loved Leo. He was kind, at heart; he was funny and good at home truths. It wasn't his fault. I simply turned my back on him in order to talk to people.

When I got home, late that evening, my dad came out and tried to move away the four girls and one boy hanging about by our garden gate. 'Here's Amy,' he said, as I stepped out of the Solar-driven car. 'She'll be tired. Excuse us.'

'We've waited all day,' one of the girls said.

'I know you have –' my dad started to say. He had an air of authority about him, but not like a father. Certainly not like my father, anyway.

'Dad,' I said, 'there's only five of them.'

They looked at me, those five, with such hope and gratitude. I was tired, yes, but then I hadn't been hanging round someone's front gate all day. The Solar influences that craved success seemed to want to reject the very people through which that success was achieved. Success, for me, if not for my dad any longer, *was* these five young people; so young, quite a bit younger than me, but people in their own right.

. 'They've all got fan-packs,' my dad said.

'How would you like to come in the house for a few minutes?' I said.

'You'll have thousands of them queuing up tomorrow,' my dad said, so loudly that some of the neighbours came to their front windows to see what all the commotion was.

'Do you still live here?' the one boy said, looking up the narrow staircase as we all came into the hall. 'I can't believe you still live here.'

'No,' said what must have been his older sister, 'not in this poky little place.'

I had to laugh at the look on my dad's face. 'Come on through to our poky little living room,' I said, leading the way. 'My dad's going to get us all some orange juice, aren't you, Dad?'

'This place is just like ours,' the boy looked and said.

'Yeah,' said his sister.

The others nodded, looking about for evidence of star status, a hidden swimming pool or doorways to the fifteen ensuite bedrooms and the maid's quarters and the built-in studio. 'This place is just like yours,' I said to them all, 'and I'm just like you.'

'No you're not,' the girls all said.

'No you're not,' my dad said, 'is she, Jill?' as my mum came in with my sisters hanging from her elbows.

'Jo and George!' one of the girls declared, running up to my famous sisters as they hid behind the business blue fabric of my mum's work skirt.

22

My mum gave me a welcome-home smile. She would have hugged me, but our little kitchen was getting too crowded to move in.

'Dad,' I said, as my mum was ushering the grateful girl and boy fans from our door, 'at least let me make a cup of tea. Let me do something.'

It was funny, how much I wanted to do the little things, iron myself a skirt, get told off for lazing in bed all morning, be made to do the washing up. All the boring, domestic things I used to avoid I somehow missed. Cars arrived to pick me up in the mornings; I never had to catch the bus. The ordinary seemed out of bounds for me now. 'Let me at least make a cup of tea, Dad,' I had to keep saying.

'I'm not having females messing up my kitchen,' he said. He used to be something in finance, I never understood quite what exactly; but then, in those days, he couldn't have boiled an egg without setting fire to the house. Now he called it 'his kitchen', which he kept immaculately clean and tidy, but with everything put away in strange places, so that nobody but he could find the teapot in the oven or the wok tucked deep under the sink. 'All the best cooks are men,' he said, 'so stay out of there.'

'Oh, leave him to it,' my mum was saying, coming back in, trying not to trip over Jo and George, who were fighting on the floor.

'Yeah,' my dad pointed with the index fingers of both his hands as if firing two guns at the girls on the floor, 'leave me to it.'

My mum gave me that hug. 'Good trip?' she said, trying to speak quietly, being drowned out by the twins as they tussled round our ankles.

'Yes, Mum,' I said, glad to be home, even though I had only been gone one day and night.

'I'm going to start going to yoga again,' my mum was saying, trying to untangle the twins. 'As soon as you get back from America, I'm going back to yoga classes.'

'America!' my dad said.

'Mum?' I said. 'Are you not – '

But my mum shook her head slightly, her face asking me not to ask her about it right now, like this. I had so wanted her to come to America with me. I could tell she wanted to talk to me properly about it, but only to tell me why she wouldn't be coming.

'America!' my dad said again, with that faraway, dreamy look that came over him whenever anyone mentioned the 'good ol' US of A.' Not that anyone but my dad ever said that.

'America! The good ol' US of A! Harley Davidson!'

'Yeah, yeah, yeah,' my mum said.

I laughed.

'I've been to Solar to talk over the schedules,' she said. Yeah, yeah, yeah.

'That explains it,' I said. She'd given up her job as a maths teacher. But dressed like that, she still looked like the teacher she was, the figure of authority I wanted on my side against Ray Ray.

'The good ol' – '

'Oh, for goodness sake!' my mum snapped. She had been a great teacher, not just a good one – and she'd given it up for me. 'Can't you take these two to bed? It's way past their time.'

Jo and George were fighting in their pyjamas. 'No!' they yelled, and ran off with my dad in pursuit. They were the famous Peppercorn twins, featured in a teen-magazine article about me that had included a big picture of them, only a couple of weeks ago.

24

'I will make that cup of tea,' I said, searching for the pot.

'You did enjoy Paris, didn't you?' my mum asked, as we waited for the kettle to boil. Above our heads, a thump, which sounded like a dead body hitting the floor.

'I'm all right,' my dad was shouting down the stairs. 'I'm all right!'

'I'm all right, too,' I said to my mum.

'Yes, you are,' she said. 'But you'll have us inundated, if you go inviting everybody in the house like that. You're not here most of the time.'

'Then I won't be doing it most of the time, will I?' I said, pouring the tea into three mugs. My mum kind of clicked as she stood behind me. From above us, twin screams as my dad crashed, trampolining from one to the other of the twins' new beds. They loved it when he did things like that.

I turned to hand her a mug of tea. 'You're not coming to America with me, are you,' I said.

She smiled. 'I can't, Amy. I tried, but the arrangements have been made.'

'What arrangements?'

'Hotels, mainly. It's too late to change all the bookings.'

'We should have done this sooner,' I said. 'I really wanted you there.'

'I know, I know. Come on, this one's okay. It'll be just you and Leo. He'll look after you. Leo's your friend, isn't he?'

'Yes. But he's – you know.'

'I know,' she smiled. 'He's Solar, through and through. You don't trust them at the moment, after – everything.'

'No,' I said, quietly, looking down at the floor.

'Amy,' she said, just as quietly, 'I'm with you. I'm here, you'll be there, but we'll still be together. Don't worry. Leo's fine. He's just as worried about you. He said you might not have enjoyed yourself, in Paris. He said –'

'When? When did you speak to Leo?'

'He called me. He was worried. He overheard you saying –'

'Mum, that's just it. He overheard me. There's always – it's a network of ears and eyes, and I can't get away from them. They're everywhere. He was listening to me talking to Beccs on the train, wasn't he? I know he was. He only heard a bit of what I said. He didn't hear it all. I was telling Beccs I wasn't expecting to enjoy myself, but I did. Leo heard the first bit only. I can't say anything, can I!'

'Amy, he was trying to help.'

'Was he? Isn't that what they always say? Isn't that how they justify trying to control my whole life?'

'Come here,' she said, holding me, 'come here. At least he was telling me. I want him to tell me.'

'He tells everyone,' I said.

'Yes,' she said, 'but if I'm included, we'll be fine, won't we? As long as I have enough information, we can play them at their own game. And win!'

She hugged me tighter. 'And win, Amy. Hear me?'

I nodded into her shoulder.

She eased me away, to look into my face. She smiled. 'When in Rome,' she said. 'It isn't me, not really. But I can play games.'

'Can you, Mum?'

'Oh, yes. And I'll tell you what, shall I? There's no better player than me, once I get going. They'll find that out, soon enough, I can assure you.'

I breathed out, easily. Another weight had just been lifted from my shoulders. My mum hugged me. She knew. She sounded like a schoolteacher when she assured me, so I felt assured. I felt safe in her arms. Ray could never get past his fear of such authority as my mum could command on her daughter's behalf.

26

*** Five

'**N**obody knows where we're going tonight,' I said to Beccs as we were looking into her dressing-table mirror. I loved getting ready to go out. Beccs and I always tried to get together to do our hair and our make-up. We were in her house, so I'd brought over a big bag of clothes for us to try on. Beccs probably wouldn't be able to wear too much of it; she and I had different tastes, as well as very different body shapes. Beccs liked nothing more than playing a good hard game of football. She was the stronger of the two of us, with much bigger ankles and wrists than mine. But we loved messing around like this.

'What is it,' she said, 'a burger-joint?' Beccs wanted to try on a pair of boots from my bag, only they wouldn't zip up over her calves. 'Football player's ankles!' she said, laughing.

We always laughed. In a way, it was a shame we were going to pick Ben up in the cab on the way to the restaurant. Beccs and I were best on our own, with no one else there to interfere with our shared sense of humour. Before, when she'd been hanging out with her cousin Kirsty a lot, I'd sometimes felt as if my funny-bone had been broken, I missed so much all the laughs we'd shared.

'No,' I said, 'it's a really nice restaurant. It's like, so exclusive, you have to book a month in advance, usually, to get a table.'

'A month?'

'Leo did it, this afternoon. He just called them up.'

'The advantages of being famous,' Beccs said. 'But I thought no one knew where we were going. Leo must do.'

'Nobody but him,' I said. 'Look, try this on.'

'With those stripes? You must be joking. I'd look like some kind of weightlifter!'

Ben was dressed entirely in black. 'Wow!' Beccs hissed from beside me in the cab. 'Look at him!'

He was smoking a cigarette, wearing a black jacket, black shirt and jeans, black boots. Only his white shirt buttons and cigarette end showed, glinting and glowing in the low street lighting. He looked sheer music-biz.

'No smoking,' the cabbie called, as Ben approached.

Ben smiled, ostentatiously flicking the cigarette sparking down the pavement. He hopped into the cab. 'Where we going, then?' he said.

'Hello, Ben,' Beccs said.

'Hi. Where we going?'

'Nobody knows,' said Beccs, 'except Amy and Leo.'

'And me,' said our cabbie, turning slightly to speak to us.

'That was so we won't be bothered,' I said.

'I'm not bothered, anyway,' Ben said.

'No,' I said, 'I know you're not. But sometimes, when I go out, if people see me –'

'She just wants to spend a quiet evening with her friends. That's all, isn't it, Amy?'

'Yes,' I said.

'She doesn't want any fuss,' Beccs said.

'Is this what you call no fuss?' Ben said, lighting a cigarette, looking from the ornate reception into the huge dining room of the restaurant, peering over a sea of heavy menus and tall wine glasses and rows and rows of knives and forks. 'This is no fuss, is it?'

'Nobody makes a fuss here,' I said.

'Cool,' Ben said, smoking.

'They'll leave us alone,' I said.

'If you'd like to follow me?' a waiter sidled up to say. Ben asked if he could have a beer. 'We'll take your order for drinks at the table,' the waiter said, gliding ahead of us.

'Wow! I'm so glad we dressed up!' Beccs said, looking her best in light blue. She'd chosen a good contrast against my cream dress. We were both wearing beads and bangles, but passed by a table full of dinner-jacketed men and ladies wearing what looked very much like real diamonds – big ones!

We laughed, Beccs, Ben and I, as we were shown to our table. I was surprised to find a long envelope with my name on it at one of the place settings. There was a single red rose. Nobody was supposed to know where we were.

'What is it?' Beccs said.

I shrugged.

'I'll have a beer,' Ben said to the waiter. The man nodded. 'They'll have some wine,' Ben said.

'No,' Beccs said. 'Orange juice for me.'

'I'll have orange, too,' I said.

'Well,' Ben said, 'it was my birthday last week, and I'm still celebrating. I'm eighteen.'

Neither Beccs nor I were quite seventeen yet. Ben had turned eighteen and we hadn't known.

'It's fantastic,' Ben grinned. 'I can do just what I like.'

'You always could,' Beccs said.

'No, now I can. I feel great. Fantastic! What's in the envelope, then?'

Ben felt great. Fantastic, he said. But something about the defiance with which he seemed to make simple statements made them sound loaded, as if he was trying to convince himself, and us, of how happy he was. He touched the crystal glasses, the tropical flowers, the elaborate place settings. He glanced up at the single rose against which my envelope rested. He kept looking at me, trying to get me to open it. 'Happy birthday, Ben,' I said.

'Yes,' Beccs smiled. She reached out and touched his hand.

He smiled, turning his hand away to touch the glasses again, the flowers, the bone-white buttons of his cuffs.

The waiter brought Ben his beer and Beccs and me our orange juice. Ben glanced at the waiter for any signs of disapproval before picking up the glass and draining at least half the beer in one go. The waiter didn't show a sign of noticing a single thing.

'Open your envelope,' Ben said, as if he'd been responsible for placing it there.

I hoped he was. He wasn't. Inside, I found the lyrics of a song, a sad song, like a poem, written to me:

Never Let You Go.

It was signed. Adam Bede.

'What is it?' Beccs asked, trying to peer over the top of the page.

I folded it back. Ben asked the waiter for another beer. He burped loudly, looking round blatantly at the other diners at another table, none of whom took the slightest bit of notice. He made me think of what Leo had said about Ben's attitude, his issues, and how badly he was dealing with them.

'A song,' I said.

'A song?' Beccs asked.

Ben didn't say anything. He shuffled the many knives and forks and spoons lined up against the edges of his place at the table.

'Just a song,' I said.

Beccs laughed. 'Who's leaving songs for you, and single red roses, at the dinner table, then? As if I didn't know!'

I had a quite a large handbag with me, much larger than the sort of thing I usually carried. Mostly I carried nothing. But today I reached down for my bag, bringing out the two gift-wrapped parcels I had for my friends. Placing the two presents on their empty place settings, I said: 'These are for you.'

They looked at them. 'What is it?' Ben said. From where I sat opposite him across the round table, I could feel his tension. His rearranged knives and forks seemed to shudder. His newly emptied beer glass rang, humming slightly under the overall bubble of the conversations from the tables all round us.

I didn't answer Ben. We both watched Beccs open her gift. 'It has picture messaging,' I said, as she opened the flap to reveal the liquid crystal display of the lively little red mobile phone. 'Yours is blue,' I told Ben, who still hadn't touched his package, but looked at it like some kind of unwelcome food item he hadn't ordered and had no intention of tasting. 'Other than the colour, all our phones are the same. We can picture-message each other.'

'Cool,' Beccs said. She leaned across and gave me a kiss on the cheek. She hardly ever did that to me. To her cousin Kirsty, yes: all the time. Kirsty used to do it to her, a lot, to demonstrate and leave me in no doubt of what good friends they were. But Beccs kissed me when she meant it. 'Open yours, Ben,' she said.

He did as he was told. 'Thank you,' he said, opening the box. 'It's – a –'

I watched his face as he stopped speaking mid-sentence. He looked at me, above me, a little to my right. Then he disappeared as someone's hands covered my eyes.

Never Let You Go
(The French Song)

I thought I saw you yesterday
You looked how you looked
When you went away.
Nothing about you has changed
Though our lives have rearranged.

I think I see you everywhere,
Same face, same smile,
Same eyes, same hair,
Exactly as you were before.
We're not together any more.

How can I forget you
When you've never gone away from me?
As I go on I cannot let you
Age a day from me –
The song of your voice, your breath in my hair,
Your face in the new sunlight,
My clothes, without yours, thrown over the chair –
I reach for you in the night –
I saw you yesterday, today, I'll see you tomorrow,
You aren't there,

But I won't let you go.
Just cannot let you go.

So much for nobody knowing where we were!

'Your man – Leo? He said I'd find you here. And here you are.' Adam Bede, dressed in jeans and leather jacket, with his long dark hair and single earring, somehow managed to seem to belong here. He was dressed like a biker, but looked relaxed and confident surrounded by the opulence of the restaurant.

'Your man, your Leo, yes, he told me. I'm going to your record company tomorrow with my manager.'

'Are you?' I said.

'So. My manager will be talking with your manager, yes? We have arranged a concert next month, huge, under the Eiffel Tower. I wanted to see you before.'

'Before the concert?'

'No,' he smiled. He glanced at Beccs and Ben. 'I'm intruding your dinner,' he said.

Beccs was smiling at him. Ben wasn't.

'No,' I said, 'sit down. Have a drink with us.'

The waiter hovered. Adam sat between Ben and me at the table. 'What have you been drinking?' he asked Ben.

'I'm sorry,' I said. 'Adam, this is Beccs Bradley, and this is Ben Lyons. Guys, this is Adam Bede.'

Adam shook their hands. 'Beer?' he said to Ben. 'We'll have beer,' he said to the waiter.

Ben decided to light another cigarette.

'Adam Bede,' Beccs said. 'From the show. Amy told me.'

'Yes,' Adam smiled. 'I wanted to give Amy my song. I would like very much for you to sing it, Amy. Do you like the words?'

'They're beautiful,' I said.

Ben dragged at his cigarette, took another mouthful from his emptying glass of beer. Adam didn't touch his drink.

'You don't mind me – finding you, like this?' Adam said.

'I'm going to kill that Leo,' I said, looking across the table at Ben.

'You do mind?' Adam said.

'No, no, I didn't mean –'

'She means she wants you to stay,' Beccs said.

But smoke blew over the surface of the table as she said it. Ben had a look about him, an attitude as he slouched in his chair, that I could imagine him using amongst the young offenders in the terror of his remand home.

Adam was receiving all the wrong messages. Ben was making me anxious. Adam was bound to feel uncomfortable. 'Maybe I will see you tomorrow?' he said.

'Yes,' I said, 'you will.'

He kissed my cheeks. 'I hope you will do my song. It will suit your voice. So, anyhow – see you.'

'Yeah,' said Ben, 'see you.'

A long, hefty silence set round us on Adam's departure. Nobody knew what to say. We sat on and on in silence until the waiter appeared to take our order for food.

'I'll have another beer with mine,' Ben said, 'as it's a celebration.'

His mouth was smiling; the rest of his face was not. There was much more happening in Ben than met the eye, or was revealed through his eyes. He was celebrating; he said so: so we had to believe him. But I couldn't help thinking he was drinking to something other than his eighteenth birthday, something much deeper and darker than that.

'Do you remember James Benton?' Beccs said, not long before she had to leave.

'Yes,' I said, 'I remember James. You must too, don't you Ben? Wasn't he in your year?'

Ben shrugged. 'I didn't know them much, did I,' he said. Ben hadn't been at our school long before – before he'd left. I'd forgotten.

Beccs looked at me, before continuing. 'James and I have been – you know – we've been going out.'

Ben didn't look up.

'Beccs!' I said, labouring not to let Ben suck out and destroy every bit of excitement Beccs and I might share.

'Not – you know – going out. But – you know – just – going out.'

'Not going out,' I laughed, 'but just going out?'

'Exactly!' she said.

We laughed. 'How long?' I said, hoping it wasn't very long at all. I hated to think of Beccs doing anything without having told me about it. She had become my anchor, keeping me attached to real life, the absolute life beyond the false star-shine of the camera-flash: the life to which I would, some day, inevitably return. I wanted to feel that attachment, that contact. I wanted an ordinary life to fall back on, when the time came.

'Not long,' said Beccs.

Of course, not long. She was my friend; if she had anything to tell me, she'd have told me.

'A week, a bit more. We've been out – a couple of times.'

'Couple of times in a week, eh?' I smiled. Beccs and I, me and Beccs would have laughed together at this. By now, on our own, we'd have been in uncontrollable fits. We understood the world best that way, laughing at everything, through everything. But with Ben there, it was different. The couple of times Beccs had been out with James Benton were times that Ben had been out with nobody. He went out, we knew, on his own. To where, we never knew. I had no doubt that it was all part of Ben trying to cope with his feelings, but he never said, so we never asked.

'How's it going at Solar, Ben?' Beccs had to say to him, trying to draw him out of himself.

'All right,' Ben said. 'Yeah, good.'

'Ben's learning the business, through and through,' I said, 'aren't you, Ben?'

He smiled. 'Yeah. Through and through. I'm going to be a record producer,' he said.

'A record producer?' Beccs said, leaning with interest into what he was saying. 'That sounds great.'

'Yeah,' Ben said. 'You get to, like, say how everything should sound. You're not doing your own songs, or anything, but working out how other people's sound best.'

'Won't you do your own songs any more then?' Beccs asked.

He looked at me. The envelope that Adam Bede had left lay open by my dessert plate. 'Anyone can write songs,' he said. 'It's getting them to sound any good that takes real skill. I can do that, I reckon.'

'I like your songs, Ben,' I said.

He glanced at the envelope again. 'Yeah? You wanna hear my latest, do you?'

'Do you have it with you?'

'I remember it. The words, that's all I have. I'll say it, like a poem, shall I? This is my latest poem:

This night tonight, had you been willing,

The dark. could have contained no scare,
No prowl and pressing silence for killing,
No breath of threat on the silent stair.'

'Killing?' I said. 'What is this?'
    'Listen!' He leaned into the table to glare at us. 'Just listen:

Had you been willing, you could have been
The glimmer of a moonlit blade,
A shivering lamp where I could've seen
The movements my assailant made.'

Ben had stood up, announcing his artistic presence to the
tables left, right, behind and in front of us. To our surprise,
he was not asked by the waiters to sit down and shut up, but
encouraged by smiles all round, by looks of interest from
diners immediately prepared to be entertained.

You could have been, if you'd been mine,
The final end of jealousy,
Clandestine, agonised decline
Of him, and the start of me.

Approaching the table to our left, Ben appealed alarmingly,
charmingly to three middle-aged, bejewelled women.

If you'd been mine I could have slain
The darkest Him without regret,
I could have knifed and knifed again
But the Devil isn't quite dead yet.

I wanted to cry out to him to stop; but on it went, verse after
verse, descending into the darkness of a murderous night-

mare, with Ben casting forward, stabbing out the cruelty of his remembered lines, his ghastly, terrible rhymes:

> *I could have slain them all my dear*
> *If you hadn't said all you have said.*
> *You didn't have to make me hear*
> *You could have left me on the bed*
> *Sleeping as though I had you near,*
> *Your arm beneath my aching head.*
>
> *But now you've made it all too clear,*
> *Now you've made the pillow red.*
> *I really had too much to fear*
> *But now I've only made you dead.*

Ben played as if to a theatre gallery, jealously guarding his audience of theatregoers from me. To the diners fresh from their West End shows, this precocious performer was a young and handsome actor delivering a beastly but beautiful piece of restaurant theatre, a one-act tragedy, going free:

> *But you look so strange just lying there,*
> *Your lips so pale, your face so grey.*
> *And I like your eyes, the way they stare,*
> *I like your crazy hair that way.*

He was like a beautiful young madman, a murderer with all the gentle, charming harm of the devil in him:

> *You love me don't you? Yes you do.*
> *No, don't tell me, I'll just know.*
> *I think I'll lie back down with you*
> *And kiss you, once, before I go.*

And he went, with a diabolical flourish, to an enthusiastic ripple of sincere applause. Ben floated back to his seat as the clapping died down. For his audience, Ben's performance had drawn to its terrible conclusion and had come to an end. For Ben, it was only just beginning; Ben started up where other people usually left off, and then he never left off.

✦✦✦ Six

Shortly after that, Beccs had to go. I wanted to go with her, to leave Ben where he was, wherever that was. I wanted to share a cab with her to hear more about her news in the way she would have told only me.

'Do you think Ben's all right?' she said to me in the loo.

'I don't know,' I said. I felt responsible for him this evening, having asked Ben to come out with us. 'I hope he is. I need to speak to him about something.'

'That's good,' Beccs said. 'Don't leave him on his own.'

'It's still early,' Ben said, as we waved Beccs away in her cab from outside the restaurant. 'We could still go somewhere.'

'Where?'

'I don't know. Why don't we go to a club?'

'I'm not old enough to go to clubs.'

'You go to clubs with the crew. You go with your fancy Leo, why not with me?'

'Who told you that? I bet Leo told you!'

Ben gave a little laugh. 'You think so?'

'What else did Leo tell you?'

'Nothing. He doesn't even speak to me. He talks to every-one but me. Why? What's the matter? What else is there to tell?'

40

'Leo tells everybody everything, one way or another. He drives me crazy, sometimes.'

'Crazy?' Ben said. 'You don't know anything about crazy.'

I was walking by his side with my jacket on and a big peaked cap pulled down low over my face. A cap was usually the last thing I'd wear, but I'd taken to carrying this one, a pink, silky jockey cap, rolled up in the pocket of my coat. The peak on it was long and wide enough to obscure most of my face if I kept looking down at the ground.

'Don't talk to me about crazy,' Ben said.

I didn't want to, either, after the grim grey horror of the lyrics of his song. 'It's a good idea for you to become a record producer, Ben,' I said.

His voice came up. 'Yeah,' he said. I wasn't talking to him about crazy, but about the opposite, the opportunity I hoped he had begun to recognise hc'd been given. 'Yeah,' he said, the flatness going out of his voice, letting me know how keen he was becoming about the idea. 'Yeah, record producer. Can't wait to lose most of my hair and grow a ponytail, get a beer-gut.'

'You'll get one of those soon enough,' I said, smiling, 'the way you're going.'

'I'm all right,' he said. 'I'm fine. They can't touch me.'

'Who can't?'

'Anybody. Nobody. Look – tell you what, let me show you something. Come with me, will you?'

'Where?' I asked, smiling, because he was suddenly frantic but positively animated all at once. Ben's excitement had always been infectious; but now his enthusiasms came and went so precipitously, his moods swinging from morose to manic so quickly I had to hold on to the highs for dear life, trying to make them last. If I didn't anchor Ben to his enthusiasms, I knew he'd be slipping away from me again, looking elsewhere for grim appreciation.

'Where are you taking me?'

'Look,' he said, fishing a big bunch of keys from his pocket. 'Look at these.'

'Keys?'

'The studios.'

'Solar?'

'Solar!'

'Ben!'

'What do you think?'

'I think they'll kill you if they find out.'

'No they won't. Big Ron knows I've got them. He says anytime, anytime I feel like it.'

And if Big Ron, the studio manager, said anytime, anytime was all right. Even Ray Ray had slightly less to say than Ron on studio time and access.

'Will you come with me? I've been working on some stuff. Amy, I'd really like you to hear it.'

We were walking through Leicester Square. It was getting late on a Friday evening. The square was packed. Nobody seemed to notice me, with the peak of my cap covering most of my face. It wasn't always easy to go out like this, if too many people saw me and wanted to speak to me. Crowds didn't always know what they were doing. A little while ago I'd been trying to get a burger, but a crowd had gathered and someone had got up on one of the burger-bar tables. The plastic table had broken and hurt somebody. I didn't want things like that to happen because of me. So I wore my huge cap, with sunglasses sometimes.

The crowds were so dense nobody could really see me

anyway, with my face at around about shoulder height.

It was great. Buskers were busking. About eight guys were playing drums, with four or five very fit looking girls dancing. Over the way, an electric guitarist was playing cover versions of hit songs.

'I've been working on stuff!' Ben enthused, dancing in front of me, walking backwards. He bumped into a bunch of celebratory girls all wearing balloons and fairy wings and things, heading in the opposite direction. 'She's coming with me!' he yelled, grinning at them.

They cheered.

'And,' he cried, 'you know who she is?'

'Don't, Ben,' I tried to say, pulling down the peak of my jockey cap. There were so many people. I shouldn't even have been there.

'You know who she is?' Ben shouted. He was happy, there and then, for that moment. I'd seen so many shifts in Ben so quickly I could see how he held on to a moment, afraid to let it go over the edge.

'Ben!' But I smiled, lifting my face.

'See her?' Ben pointed, looking at the girls. 'See? Amy Peppercorn! How about that then!'

They saw me. I saw their moment of recognition. But I also saw Ben. He was proud of me. Ben Lyons was looking at me in the way he'd used to before he'd committed car crimes. He'd had a few beers in belated celebration of his eighteenth birthday, but so what? Energy like Ben's flickers with such force, such brilliance when it's on, that you never want to see it switched down again.

'Hey!' one of the girls shouted. Another screamed. I don't think they were fans, particularly, but they were screamers, girls out together in the West End for a screaming good time.

'It *is* Amy Peppercorn!' another shrieked.

Other people stopped. The crowd around us grew. Ben pulled me into the space the drummers and dancers had claimed for themselves. He whipped off my cap. The drummers stepped it up, putting out a fantastic beat none of us could resist. One of the girls kissed me. They danced with me. Ben disappeared. He came back carrying the electric guitarist's amplifier, pulling the guitarist himself along by his amp lead. Ben set him up. He started on a rhythm riff that blended in with the drummer's up-beat, and the crowd went wild.

One of the girl dancers screamed. She did it like I do it, screaming at the crowd. Everyone was clapping. People were climbing onto the railings of the square. I saw a face appear through the leaves and branches of a plane tree. I was laughing, dancing with Ben. He looked happier than I had ever seen him, *ever*. The drummers and the dancers were putting on a show for their biggest ever audience. Leicester Square was packed solid. Those people at the back couldn't have known what was going on, only that it was something big.

And it was! I was coming alive. The drums were beating a track into my pounding heart. Suddenly, and everything good around me seems to be sudden, I felt right there, at one with the dancers and the crowd. We were so close to them. This was truly live. No professional karaoke here. Nothing was pre-recorded, rehearsed or in any way anything but spontaneous. This, in many ways, was the best way to put on a live performance. The crowd, the audience, had not chosen to come and see me. I could communicate here with those people who, at any other time, would have seen me as just another pop face on the Friday night *Toppas* telly.

The same girl screamed. I screamed. We screamed at each other. There were no V formations of dancers, but real street-performers responding in the way the music deserved.

The guitarist started to pick out the tune to one of my old songs, *The Word On The Street*. I started to sing:

The word is out there
The word on the street
There is no doubt there's
A life so incomplete

Ben laughed. Life didn't feel incomplete, not for us, at this moment. Ben had suffered, so had I: but not now, either of us.

There is no doubt there's
A life so incomplete
When you're not about where
We always used to meet
But now the word is on the street

My love, you're back
And our love's back on the right track

The guitarist fell into the rhythm of the song as the drums pounded out an appropriate backbeat. They went on. They went on.

My love, you're back
And our love's back on the right track
Now the word is on the street.

'The word's on the square, too!' Ben cried, laughing. We wheeled through the dancers, me singing, the other girls chanting. Shivers were running up my spine. This was working. Ben would be healed. He'd be free of his guilt, and I'd be through with the last vestiges of regret over Jag.

'Nobody else could do this!' Ben shouted at me.

I sang into the crowd. Everybody seemed to know *The Word*. Soon they were singing it with me. They knew me, these people. Even those that hadn't, before that night, wouldn't forget. I fell in love with them. All my emotions came welling up. I jumped up into the air; I felt like I was floating above the space we'd created, Ben and I, watching what was happening as if I was in the trees with those other moon faces staring down into the square.

The stars were out above the trees. A camera flash obliterated everything for a moment. Only for a moment. This was fantastic! I was hooked on this. I never wanted it to end.

But it didn't last long, as the police beat a path through what must have seemed to them like a troublesome crowd. So many officers had converged so quickly, along with a surprising number of press representatives. We'd be a riot in the Sunday papers in the morning, I knew. We could have been arrested, Ben and me, for incitement. I wouldn't have minded. It would have been worth it. I'd have enjoyed it perhaps, being taken into custody with Ben, to show him that I could experience at least a little of what he'd been through.

But nobody was arrested. The police moved everybody on, for their own safety, bringing them down from the railings and trees. They stopped the drums and the guitarist, nodding good-naturedly at me, ignoring Ben.

The girl dancers hugged me. 'It must be great to be

you,' one said. She smiled into my face. I was made of love. 'Yeah,' she said, feeling everything I had inside from reading what was written on my face, 'it must be really great to be you.'

Seven

It was really great, being me. It *was*. When people said these things, real people speaking spontaneously to me about what they imagined I was, it made it much greater being me than just – than just being me! I wasn't who I thought I was then, but what people like that lovely girl in Leicester Square said I was. I liked and preferred it that way. If I could always feel like this, I'd never lose contact with the people the Solar know-alls would have had me walk straight through. The celeb-rags and the nastier newspapers couldn't interfere, with what they'd try to say about me. It was really great being me.

Ben seemed to think so, too. 'Was that fantastic, or what?' he was saying, opening the Solar studios.

'Yeah,' I said, 'it's what it's all about.'

'I'm glad you think so,' he said. 'Things like that, they don't happen to everyone.'

'Ben,' I said, as we walked into the darkened studio, 'do you think we should be here, like this?'

He snapped on a switch by the door. The cold strip-lights flickered, blinking and buzzing the disused room into view. 'Come on,' he said. 'Don't worry about it. Big Ron knows, I told you. We'll be fine. Come on. This is great.'

He dashed over to the control console, switching more things on, turning dials. The sound equipment started to hum. 'Listen!' he cried. 'Remember that?'

I laughed. 'I remember that.' He was talking about the time when we had been putting our school band together. Ben had chosen the name of the band, Car Crime. He had been the initial driving force; but he and I had shared the same excitement, the same sense of anticipation on just hearing the hum of the amplifiers. 'I remember everything,' I said.

'So do I,' he said, with just a flicker of regret. 'Yeah. Listen. I've been laying down a few tracks. Backing stuff, mainly. See what you think.'

The place was deserted but for the two of us. Ben's music started up, beating out a sound that tried to fill the empty spaces, attempting to bring the studio back to the life it was meant to lead. Ben was dancing about. He looked desperate to appear happy. He looked desperate.

I was trying to be happy for him.

'What do you think?' he shouted over the blurred loudness of sound he was intent on assaulting us with.

I nodded, moving, not dancing. There was something about the driven, frantic hysteria of the sound of Ben's music now, a desperation that would not be danced along with. Maybe his songs had always been like this, and I simply hadn't noticed? Now it seemed to want too much, to be asking too much, demanding, without the least bit of subtlety or charm. It was quite well put together, but missed its mark. However much I wanted to be moved, to be touched or excited by these sounds, all they did was try to batter me into submission.

'You like?' he shouted at me.

I nodded again, moving, trying to dance against the brash wall of drum and bass and more bass and ever more frantic drum. The music was trying too hard. Ben was dancing, also trying too hard. I felt he didn't feel as inspired to make music as he once had been. Now his music didn't truly inspire him to dance, so he had to try, and he tried too hard.

We pretended, the pair of us, making the effort for long minutes on end without looking at each other. There was, there could be no contact with the truth coming out for examination like this. We would admit to nothing. The Solar silence under the noise we were making showed, in the tilt of a disused, broken music stand, in the stilled mixing decks, the unspoken honesty we were both about to have to face at the end of Ben's recording. We moved, both of us, but waited for the reverberating pause, the absence of sound that we were going to have to fill with words.

'What do you think, really?' he said eventually, filling in with words, waiting for whatever words in return.

I fought for something to say. Nothing came.

'Yeah,' he said. 'I told you, it's background stuff, mainly. It's not – I need – something else, don't I?'

'Some more practice, perhaps?' I managed to say.

'No,' he said. 'I was better before. I was good, then. Don't say I wasn't.'

'I wasn't going to.'

'I've lost it.'

'No you haven't, Ben. You haven't.'

'What, then?'

'You need – I don't know. Just wait a while. Leo says you just need to keep out of people's way for a while and – '

'Leo? What's it got to do with Leo?'

'Nothing. He's just – '

'What? He's just what? What does he know about me?'

'Nothing.'

'Well then. He wants to stay out of my way, that's all. I'm not – I can do stuff!'

'I know you can, Ben.'

'I could do – that letter from that bloke, tonight. That song. Let me have a go at it.'

'It's his song, Ben.'

'Yeah, but I could have a go, couldn't I? Why, don't you want me to, or something?'

'You can –'

'Let me see it, then.'

'What, now?'

'Now. Why not? Now.'

'Okay. No reason why not.' I went into my big handbag. 'Here,' I said, handing him the envelope that Adam Bede had left me. 'Here, take it.'

Ben was looking at me as if he hadn't expected to be handed Adam's song as easily as that. He took it tentatively, with his eyes still fixed on mine. Then he turned and sat at the studio control console, opening the envelope, starting to read:

Never Let You Go

I thought I saw you yesterday
You looked how you looked
When you went away.
Nothing about you has changed
Though our lives have rearranged.

He looked up at me, then down.

I think I see you everywhere,
Same face, same smile,
Same eyes, same hair,
Exactly as you were before.
We're not together any more.

'It's – ' he said, looking back at me. He looked down again, saying nothing.

'What?' I said.

'Nothing,' he said. Then said nothing. He just held onto the page, grasping it too tightly, creasing it at the edges.

'Ben?'

Nothing. Creased edges. Then nothing.

'Ben. What is it?'

'"I think I see you everywhere, same face, same smile, same eyes, same hair,"' he said, as if reading, but without reading.

'Ben, it's nothing to do with you, or us. It's different. Everything's changed. It has to. That's what happens.'

'This is crap!' he suddenly snapped, tearing the paper, ripping it in two. He threw it in my direction. It fell far short of me, flapping in two parts onto the floor between us. Ben was looking at me. 'You don't know what it's like,' he said.

I had to just look at him. He was probably right: how could I know? I felt what I felt. He was different; his experience was even sharper, harder than my own. This was not the same person I had known at school. This was not even the same person who had danced and smiled in Leicester Square earlier that evening.

'I can't hold onto anything,' he said.

'Ben, don't. You drank all that beer. It isn't –'

'It isn't anything! Amy, nothing's anything. It's terrible. There's always, always that – that – that thing! There's a thing, like a feeling – not like a feeling. More solid than that. I can't get away from it. Amy, I can't. I've tried.'

I went towards him.

'Don't,' he said.

For a moment I thought he was going to push me away. He didn't. I had to hold him while he struggled to get it all out, to expel the more solid something from his heart. But he couldn't do it. I felt his body wracked with anguish, his unforgiving tenseness tight in his back and labouring shoulders as he fought with himself. He was losing the fight, beating himself up and down, looking for a forgiveness trigger or button in his belly somewhere that would finally let him off. Nobody now blamed him but he himself. He was his own worst enemy: for the first time in my life I fully understood that saying. Nobody else was as hard on or as nasty to Ben as Ben.

He cried as I held him. I suppose I was able to give him that, at least. Crying's not a bad thing. It's good, usually. I wasn't doing any of it, not now, but it was good that Ben could. If this was the first time he'd cried, maybe he could start to put up a bit of a better fight?

'I'm sorry,' he said, against the side of my face. 'I keep doing this. I'm up and down, all over the place.'

'It's all right, Ben. You should let it out.'

'It doesn't come out,' he said. 'It never comes out. I can't get rid of it, Amy.'

'You need help.'

'You can help me.'

'Me?'

'You can. Don't let me go.'

'Ben, I –'

'You were a part of what happened.'

'Ben, no.'

'Take some of it. You could take some of it, couldn't you?'

Then, before I could move away, Ben tried to kiss me. 'Ben! No!'

'Why does everyone have to be against me all the time?' he was asking, as I pulled away, walking backwards from him, putting some safe distance between us.

'Why?' he was saying.

He'd kissed me, once, a long, long time ago, years perhaps, it felt, one unfortunate boy's lifetime ago. Geoff Fryer had been killed in a stolen car that Ben was driving. Our old band wasn't called Car Crime for nothing. Ben had kissed me before the fatal accident. It could have been me in that car with him. Ben knew that, as well as I did. 'Nobody's against you, Ben,' I said.

'They are! You don't know! You have no idea what people are like!'

'Ben, you need help.'

'Help? Who's going to help someone like me? You? You won't even go near me now – see what I mean?'

'You need help, Ben,' I said, stepping away from him, 'but I can't give it to you.'

He was glaring at me. His face was glowing.

'And I don't know who can' I said. 'I only wish I did.'

***Eight

All the old feelings came flooding back in. My mind kept going over and over every incident that had brought Ben and me to that moment last night. In that moment, I had looked into his eyes and seen, as if looking backwards through a time-telescope, the dreadful sequences screeching away from us in reverse, a terrible, bloody car crash unravelling from violence to order, bending metals straightening, shattered glass reintegrating, two figures seen darkly intact driving recklessly the wrong way down a dark alley. Ben was forever and forever rewinding his worst memory, wishing for a second chance back there, a place that time would not let him revisit but memory relived time and time again. But time was never time again. There were no hindsight what-ifs. Ben could never stop it now, the car crime, the crash, the consequences: I could see them in his eyes.

He made me feel that we were no further from that point, either of us; that we had not progressed one moment beyond that point of no return. It was still there, like a zero hour into which everything plummeted and then went nowhere.

Certainly, he still looked as bad, next day. As soon as I saw Ben I wondered if he had been home at all. The studios were back to their everyday bustle, but Ben looked as static and alone as the broken music stand that had witnessed the silence at the end of Ben's music last night.

He needed help; that much had become obvious. As soon as I could I was going to call Beccs to ask her what she thought we could do – if we could do anything. I'd begun to doubt that we could.

Ray Ray came down to try to motivate people; which usually meant threatening everyone in one way or another. He was being quite mild today, though, by his standards. The studio boys were recording some of the other Solar artists this morning. A new girl band called the Static Cats were rehearsing moves they wouldn't need in a recording studio. Ray would usually have geared up into red-shift by now, if I had been involved. But he didn't seem particularly concerned this time, just watching the three new girls running through their hopelessly optimistic routines. Ray had seen it all before, his haggard face said. Ray say, even when Ray say nothing. Hopeless optimism tired him out, as the three Static Cats tried and failed to impress. Maybe they were somebody else's project?

'Upstairs,' Ray finally decided to say to me, 'in my office. Twenty minutes? Adam Bede, his manager, this morning. Good for us, a cultural exchange. You sing a song of his, he launches a single here. You sing at his Eiffel Tower concert, we release a single there. Good?'

Behind us, the Static Cats were wailing. Ray looked over his shoulder. He gave a little wince. Ben was hooking himself up to headphones next to Big Ron. Leo was being wheeled in to play the synthesizer. Somebody else's project was, I could see Ray say, without him saying anything, doomed to failure. Already, in my short, ballistic career, I had seen so many come, so many go on Ray's say-so. Ray say. So!

I pictured myself, when Car Crime had first come here, believing that the No. 1 A & R man actually wanted to see us. All that hopeless optimism! I had been so lucky. Yes, I had a voice. But so what? There are thousands of us with good singing voices. Who was I that all this should have happened for me? Lucky, that was all. There were so many other talented young people who never got a break. Or even worse, there were those like the Static Cats who, having come this far, would have the cruel door of failure suddenly slammed unceremoniously in their faces. How would they cope with such rejection? So many people wanted to be where I was, cutting new songs for a second album, arranging to perform for the radio and TV slots open to me in the US, swapping songs with a French star in a pop cultural exchange across the English Channel. Yes, I was lucky. Things had certainly gone my way. Ray didn't always necessarily make it happen, but it had happened. He didn't like it that way, but accepted success with as total a lack of grace as he would have hated failure.

Just last night, I was celebrating how great it was to be me. This morning, looking at Ben's tired face between the giant earphones clamped to either side of his head, and I was wondering how long I could expect my luck to last. Not that much longer, surely?

Surely not.

But all was yet well, as Adam Bede and his manager confirmed, beaming at me in the office of my smiling manager. Ray looked truly dangerous. I felt safer with him when he was in a red-shifted huff. At least then we all knew where we stood. Smiling, Ray could mean anything, from very good to frighteningly awful.

We were good this morning, though. Agreements had been made between Ray and Adam's manager, subject to certain contractual details. I never knew what the details were. Ray made everyone too afraid to ask. I'd still try to ask, sometimes, but on this occasion I wasn't worried. Adam was very nice, kissing me on both cheeks with a Frenchman's panache rather than Leo's music-biz showmanship.

'You seen the song?' Ray champed, his sneer of a smile as cold as they come.

I nodded.

'Like it?'

'Yes,' I said. 'Very much.'

'You like to sing?' Adam's manager asked.

'Yes, I do,' I said.

'No,' Adam said, 'Pierre means would you like to sing it? To release it as a single, in France, maybe here?'

'Of course I would,' I said. 'But I've only seen the words.'

'Ah,' Adam said, 'I will sing for you.'

'You will fall in love,' his manager, Pierre Piatta, said.

I laughed. Adam's manager Pierre was so nice; a beautifully friendly man, a gentle, funny person with long dark hair and such sleepy eyes he reminded me of a great koala bear.

'Gentlemen,' Ray said, 'good business, I think. Drink?'

'Show me your – ah –' Adam said, to me, 'how do you call it – studio?'

'I'll show you the studios,' I said.

Adam wanted to sing the song for me. We'd been watching Ben trying to impress Big Ron with his pile-driven music, attempting to superimpose his signature on the sound that the Static Cats made. Adam and I had moved into another part of the studio, soundproofed from the rest, but still able to see and be seen through double or triple-glazed round sound-windows.

'I will sing the song for you now?' Adam was saying.

I glanced through to Ben, as he threw off the headphones from either side of his flaming red face. 'Yes,' I said.

'Okay,' Adam said. 'Okay.'

He started to sing *Never Let You Go*:

I thought I saw you yesterday
You looked how you looked
When you went away.

As he sang, I glanced again and again beyond him to where Ben was speaking, or perhaps shouting. Adam was singing those soft, tender words into Ben's angry spitting mouth. They went through the song together, contrasted one against the other across the scattered rooms of the Solar studios. I could see a trio of Static Cats clawing the walls on the other side from Ben, with Leo standing up as if about to run away and tell on someone to someone stronger. Leo could always find someone stronger to tell.

But Ben seemed to stop when he spotted me, with Adam singing behind me. Leo stopped when Ben did, his attention fixed on him.

Adam sang:

Nothing about you has changed
Though our lives have rearranged.

I think I see you everywhere,
Same face, same smile,
Same eyes, same hair,
Exactly as you were before.
We're not together any more.

Ben saw him singing it. The Static Cats weren't singing at all now, glancing warily at each other, trying to guess what was expected of them next. Big Ron seemed dumbfounded, which was the first time I'd seen anything affect Ron, anything.

I watched Ben, his face, the fighting anguish he showed as he walked from the room that he was in to where we were. Adam was still singing as Ben entered:

I think I see you everywhere,
Same face, same smile,
Same eyes, same hair,
Exactly as you were before.
We're not together any more.
How can I just let you
Become someone I just used to know?
As I go on I'll never forget you.
I'll never let you go.

The song ended. Ben stood in the doorway. Adam looked towards him. 'Ah,' he said, 'from last night. How are you?'

'Are you doing that?' Ben demanded.

'Ben!'

'Is something –' Adam tried to say.

'You're doing that – that crap!'

'Ben, you can't –'

'I can! I tore it up. Where is it?' he said, stalking towards Adam. 'Where is it?'

'What?'

I rushed between them. Ben reached easily above my head and pushed Adam on the shoulder. Adam did nothing but look at him. Ben pushed him again.

Big Ron appeared and dragged Ben away. Ben wasn't looking at Adam, or at me or Ron; he was looking at the floor, but staring into himself as everyone watched what was happening to him without really seeing what was happening to him. I could see some of what he was going through, more than most. The Static Cats saw some kind of unaccountable incident, Big Ron a jealous ex-boyfriend; Leo, from where he stood, saw the danger he himself had seen in Ben. Out of everyone there, it was Leo who had first detected the problems and issues Ben was struggling against, the potential, seething violence in him. It was Leo who, as he watched through the window, had decided to get something done about Ben.

✳✳✳ Nine

Adam was fine. Big Ron was all right; he'd dealt with every kind of 'crazy pumped-up spook' in his time, he said. Big Ron was big, slow and strong; nothing fazed him: he'd seen it all.

So had Leo. That was the trouble. Leo had seen everything. Adam and Ron said they'd say nothing about what had happened. Adam was fine; he was lovely, in fact. In fact, if I hadn't been smarting from Jag, I might have found Adam very, very interesting. But I was in no position, emotionally, to be that interested in anyone. That's what Ben had failed to see. But Ben, at the moment, couldn't see any further than his own blighted, tattered emotions.

Leo could, that was the trouble. 'Don't tell on him, Leo,' I said. 'Please. Ray doesn't have to know about this.'

Lovely Leo touched his curly hair, his elbows tucked protectively into his sides, one figurative finger poised at his pouted lips.

'Leo, give him a chance. He's suffering.'

'So we all have to?' Leo said.

'No,' I said, 'you shouldn't have to.'

'He's unstable, Lovely. It's too stressful to work with, for everyone.'

'I know,' I said. 'I do know. I'll get him some help. He needs help, that's all. He isn't like that underneath. Ben's so talented –'

'Oh, really?' Leo nodded, sarcastically.

'No, he is. Please, Leo. You don't have to say anything to Ray. Nobody else will.'

'Well they should.'

'No they shouldn't. It wouldn't do anybody any good. Leo, please, for me? Do it for me?'

Leo was tutting, looking up at the ceiling.

'Leo, Lovely. Please?'

He tutted again.

'Pretty-please, dear, sweet, Lovely Leo?'

'You'll get me hung,' he said.

'No, I won't. Nobody'll know. You can keep a secret, Leo, I know you can.'

'I'm not so sure, myself,' he said. 'But I'll try.'

'Oh, Leo, you're a – '

'Please, Lovely,' he said, holding up his hands, 'I know what I am. I'm a fool, that's what I am.'

'No you're not.'

'I'm a fool, I am. But, listen to me, one more incident, and I can't keep it to myself. Do we understand one another?'

'Perfectly, Lovely,' I said.

He wafted me away, flipping two limp hands. 'Get from my sight, before I scream. Just you make sure you're ready for America, that's all, my Sweet. Next week, already. Be ready, already. Are you ready?'

'I'm ready,' I said, although, of course, I wasn't.

'I'm not sorry,' Ben said, turning a hostile eye towards me. 'I'm fed up with being sorry. I've had enough of it.'

'But Ben – '

'I don't need any help. Especially not from your dad!'

My dad had said he knew a man, a counsellor. 'He helped me sort my head out,' my dad said, his thinning hair sticking up and out, his high forehead imprinted with a massive red-raw disk like a love bite from someone with a saucer for a mouth. One of the twins had stuck a toy with a big suction pad onto his head. When he tried to take the toy off, it wouldn't release. My mum had had to slide the blade of a thin knife gently between the rubber suction pad and my dad's skin. He'd popped out, but with a great disk on his face that would probably last for weeks.

'He helped me get my head sorted out,' he said, looking as if someone had just rubber-stamped him as a reject, 'when I lost my job. Don't know what I would have done without him.'

'I didn't know you'd been to a therapist, Dad,' I said.

'I know,' he said. 'Jo and George knew, but they kept it to themselves, didn't you, girls? If you like, we could try to get Ben and him together?'

'I don't think he'll want to know.'

'Oh, I think he will.'

'What makes you think so?'

'Oh,' he said, 'because of what I know this therapist can do. I'll speak to him. We'll find a way of persuading Ben.'

'Ben,' said Jo.

'Ben,' my dad said.

'Ben,' said George.

'Ben,' said I, because I knew my dad wasn't really likely to convince him, 'you need help.' Ben had stopped knowing himself; that's how I knew my dad was right about trying to get the therapist involved, but wrong about anyone's ability to persuade Ben. 'You need help, Ben.'

'Ben?' my mum had said. 'What's wrong with him?'

What could I say? What was wrong with Ben? 'He's suffering,' I said. 'Things keep happening, whenever he's around.'

'He's not dangerous, is he?'

'Is he?' my dad had said.

'Ben,' I said, 'someone has to help you with your suffering.'

'Suffering?' he said. 'Who says?'

'I say,' Beccs said, to me, 'you should go ahead and put him together with your dad's shrink.'

I laughed. 'Counsellor,' I said. 'My dad's not mad.'

'Neither is Ben,' Beccs said.

'I'm not a nutter, you know,' Ben said.

'Ben,' I said, along with everyone else.

'Ben.'

'I'm not some kind of a nutter.'

'No, I know, but people are getting –'

'People? What people?'

'Oh – just – at Solar –'

'People? Who? Ron? Your greasy Frenchman?'

'No, they're fine.'

'Who, then?'

'Me, for one. I'm worried about you.'

'Then don't be. Is that it? People? Just you?'

'No, not just me.'

'Who? Leo?'

I didn't say anything.

'Oh, yes,' Ben smirked. 'I've seen the way he keeps look-ing at me, watching me all the time. He –'

'He thinks you're trouble, Ben.'

'He thinks that, does he?' he said, taking out a box of cig-arettes. 'Well, maybe I am, but Ray doesn't seem to think so.'

'Ray?'

Ben flipped open a lighter. 'Yeah, Ray. Ray Ray. You know him?' he sneered through exhaled smoke. 'I told Ray what happened. Someone had to; I thought it should be me. So you can stop worrying – and you and your lovely Leo can butt out and leave me alone, can't you.'

*** Ten

'**A**re you ready for America?' Leo asked me.

'Are you?' I asked back, over the lunch I had asked him to have with me.

I had my pink peaked cap on and we were sitting in the little café not far from the Solar offices. We didn't often do things like this, Leo and me. He hardly ever ate during the day.

'It's okay for you,' he'd flap. 'Look at you. You're young. Believe me, Sweet, at my age, half a lettuce leaf hangs about my midriff like a Cornish pasty belt.'

Leo always made me laugh. He was slight, with a narrow waist and thin legs, not an ounce of fat on him.

'Not an ounce,' he announced to the waitress as she stood poised over our lunch table, 'not an ounce of fat, she says. Look at her,' he instructed the young waitress. She looked.

'Are you her?' she said.

'No,' Leo interjected. 'Actually, no, she is not. She is she, if you must know. I'd like a green salad, with water. Still water, if you please.' He turned to me 'Bubbles in water always make me feel as if I'm drinking someone's Jacuzzi,' he said.

The waitress stood looking at me. 'And I'll have –'

'And this young lady will have the same,' Leo said.

'Yes,' I said, 'but this young lady will have some tuna and some bread with her salad, and a glass of fresh orange juice.'

'You're her, aren't you,' the girl said, having written nothing on her pad.

'If you could just – ' Leo started to say.

'Leo,' I said. 'Please, not now. Yes,' I said to the girl, 'if you're asking me am I Amy?'

'You are.'

'Oh yes,' Leo said, 'so you are.'

'Leo,' I said again. I smiled at our waitress. 'Did you get my order?'

She looked at her blank pad, bemused. 'Yes,' she leapt, scribbling, crossing, dotting. 'Yes, I – my name's Mia, by the way. I'm your waitress.'

'Oh, really?' Leo tilted, leaning away from her. 'You're our waitress, are you?'

'Thanks, Mia,' I smiled.

She left us reluctantly, as if she'd forgotten what it was she wanted to say to me. Leo had always instructed me to walk on by, not to engage with people all over the place, all the time; but right now he seemed to have lost his patience, to be more sarcastic and unforgiving with strangers than usual. He seemed more than usually nervous, under a great strain.

'Are you ready for America?' he asked.

'Are you?'

He glanced aside, as if looking for our waitress. 'Lovely,' he said, 'I cannot tell you how much I –'

But his mobile phone started to ring. Perhaps ring was not quite the right word to describe the sound that Leo's mobile made. The flurry of lilting notes faded as if into the past, only to repeat the present before the next fade, flurry, fade. It was the prettiest ring tone I had ever heard. Leo fished out the phone from his shoulder bag, snapping it open, glancing once again in the direction taken by our retreating waitress.

'Yes!' he snapped. 'Hello? – What? Who? – I – no,' he said, glancing at me, shaking his head slightly. 'No, I can't – I'm – with a client at the moment. No. You'll have to excuse me,' he snapped, shutting down the line, switching off the pure pink phone altogether before dropping it, as if it had grown too hot or heavy, into the open gape of his brushed leather bag. 'These people,' he said.

'Who was it?'

But Leo just shook his head, looking left, waitress-bound, as if he was suddenly very hungry for his meagre green salad and still prison-water. 'Oh, you know, people. Whoever. Whatever.'

We stopped talking. Not speaking, for Leo, was a very rare thing indeed. Watching him, I was starting to wonder why his eyes were missing me so regularly, and why we were now enduring such awkward silences, like strangers trying to find something to say to each other. Leo was never, ever short of something to say. Leo just said things, whatever occurred to him, whenever he felt like it.

'You said you were looking forward to America,' I reminded him.

He seemed to sigh. 'Oh my, yes – oh dear, listen to me. Did I sound too much like Judy Garland then? Forgive me.'

I laughed. 'Who's Judy Garland?' I said.

Leo gasped exaggeratedly. 'How could you! Judy Garland? Lovely Liza's mum?'

I shook my head, none the wiser.

'Oh, my!' he declared, with one comically melodramatic hand touching his cheek. 'Lions and tigers and bears, oh my! She really doesn't know! Sweet, we must, we really must spend more quality time together.'

'We'll be together in America.'

'Yes,' he leaned across the table to squeeze my hand. 'And

I can't tell you – I'm so, so very – what am I? Lovely, I'm tired.'

'Tired?'

'Fed-up. Sick and tired of – being English!'

I laughed. 'What's wrong with being English?'

'Oh, dear,' he slumped, dropping back into his chair. 'It's such a – if only I were French. Like Adam. Or Italian. Yes, Italian. Such passion. The English, what are we? Repressed speechless one minute, the next compassionless and threatening, fighting fire with fire until everything's burnt brown and singed and useless – what's this?' he practically shouted at the poor waitress as she placed two large glasses of fresh orange juice in front of us on the table. 'What on earth is this supposed to be?'

The girl straightened stiffly in alarm.

'Leo,' I said.

'I really do believe I said still water,' he insisted, speaking into the poor girl's face. 'Would you have me as fat as Churchill?' he yapped up at her. 'Would you?'

She looked quite afraid. But, I thought, suspected, so, in a way, was Leo. He was making her afraid because someone had frightened him somehow, and fear passes on like that, from one person to another, in one way or another. 'Churchill?' the girl said, not out of curiosity, but fear.

'Churchill! Churchill! Have you never –'

'Leo!' I interjected. 'Lots of people don't know who Churchill was. Now stop it! Please, Leo. I don't want to be here with you like this – I'm sorry, Mia,' I said to the waitress. 'He ordered still water. Forgive him. He's not usually like this.'

'That's all right,' she said. But both Leo and I knew that it was not all right at all, not with so much fear circulating round and round, like fire fighting with fire.

* * *

Our waitress couldn't always have been as bad as she seemed to us, or she'd surely have been fired long ago. As it was, Leo's green salad came heaped with as much tuna and mayo and sweetcorn as my own. Leo was livid. He accused the poor girl of conspiring with his enemies.

All I wanted was to enjoy myself. It was supposed to be really great to be me. Everyone thought so. Even I did, between the bouts of trouble I had dealing with all those others, these troubled people fire-fighting one another.

'I'll eat your tuna, Leo,' I said. 'You just eat your salad.'

'That's not the point,' he said.

'What is then?'

Leo looked up.

'It's not this,' I said, indicating his tuna-filled salad plate. 'Leo, I know you better than that. What is the point, Leo? Tell me.'

He sighed. Leo was a great sigher. He was a tutter, too. He sighed and tutted. 'The point is, Lovely,' he said, 'that sometimes Leo gets sick and tired of being blamed for everything. That's what the point is.'

'I'm sorry, Leo. I shouldn't have – '

'No,' he said. 'No. It doesn't matter. You're just about to say you shouldn't have stopped me telling Ray what happened, I know you are. But it doesn't matter. I'd be blamed for what happened, or blamed for not telling him what happened, one way or the other.'

'But how can he blame you for what happened? It wasn't your fault, any of it.'

He sighed again. 'Sweet,' he said, his voice falling to not

much more than a whisper, 'shall I tell you a little secret? Shall I?'

He was looking into my eyes. I nodded. Mia bustled by, trying not to get too close.

Leo glanced at her before looking back into my eyes. 'Let me tell you something about Mr Raymond Raymond. Like all good megalomaniacs –'

'Megalomaniac?'

'Yes. Totally self-centred dictators – like all good megalomaniacs, Ray is scared.'

'Scared?'

'He's afraid.'

'Of what?'

Leo laughed, a brief snort. 'My Lovely, of everything. Of everyone. Ray Ray is afraid of everyone. He's afraid of you –'

'Me?'

'You, Sweet. He's afraid of you. He's afraid of all his artists. He's afraid of Big Ron. He's afraid of all the studio people, the session musicians, everyone. All except –'

He stalled, examining the tuna, mayo and sweetcorn mound on the side of his plate, prodding it with a fork.

'All except?' I said.

He tutted, softly, quietly. 'Don't you know? He's afraid of everyone with talent, everyone with knowledge or skill. Those things are out of his control. Oh, he'll manipulate everyone, but the very thing they have that he and his success depend upon is what he most fears. So the greater your success, the greater his fear and loathing of you. You cannot win Ray over – and neither can I. Because I'm just about the only one in the world he doesn't fear. He doesn't fear me because with me he can do what he likes, and he knows it. I'm trapped. I can't win. Whatever I do, I can't win.'

'Oh, Leo,' I said. 'Oh, dear sweet Leo.'

'No, don't,' he said, stopping me from getting up and going round to his side of the table. 'It's all right,' he said, trying to smile. 'I'm fine. I just wanted you to see how it is when your friend goes to Ray with tales of what happened. Ray comes to the person he's least afraid of in the whole world and lays blame. He always does it.'

'Then why do you – '

But Leo's face stopped me from asking him why he stood for it. Leo's face told me the answer before I could ask the question.

'I hate him,' he said, although he and I knew equally well, and his face said he meant love, not hate. Love.

When we got back to the Solar offices, Sandy, the receptionist, bombarded Leo with telephone messages. 'I told them to try your mobile,' she said, 'but they kept calling back here. Someone called Barry Bone, six times, at least. Look, three different numbers you can call him on.'

Leo took the messages and ostentatiously dumped them into Sandy's waste paper basket. 'Let them fight their own fires,' he said. 'Everything's burnt brown anyway.'

Sandy was looking at me. I shrugged.

'Let's just go to America,' I whispered, as Leo and I went into the building.

'The good ol' US of A,' he said, smiling. He squeezed my hand again. 'Lovely,' he said, 'Let's just go.'

***** Eleven

The studios were unusually quiet. One or two sound technicians threw cables from one end of the corridor and back again. They did this whenever there was nothing to do, to make them look as if they had something to do.

Leo tinkered along a keyboard, as a preliminary to the song rehearsals we'd agreed to do between us this afternoon. He started to sing one of his songs:

'*Where the bee sucks there suck I,*' he sang, but quietly, without any of his normal outrageous delivery.

I laughed, trying to put some fun back into being with him. 'Your songs always make me laugh, Leo.'

'My songs? Sweet, don't you know who wrote that one? That was Shakespeare, Lovely.'

'Oh,' I said, 'him.'

Leo laughed now. 'Indeed, Sweet. Him.'

'You know, Leo,' I said, 'it's supposed to be so great, being me, but I feel so – stupid, sometimes.'

'Stupid?'

'As if I shouldn't be here. I should be at school, finishing my education.'

'Shakespeare?' he smiled. 'I thought you were studying maths and physics.'

'And biology,' I said.

'So,' he said, cocking his head, 'what makes you think

you're not finishing your education right now? How much have you learned, in the past few months?'

'Nothing, I think. All the wrong things.'

'Come here,' he said. 'Come here, come here. Big hug! We're a pair, aren't we?'

'It's not us,' I said. 'It's all those others.'

'Ah,' he said, 'tell me about it – no, don't tell me about it. I know, Sweet. Don't you worry. Everything's fine.'

'Is it, Leo?' I said, stepping away from him, trying to see into him for reassurance beyond the words that fought fire with fire for him lately, as I had never seen him so fired, fired up, so fiery. 'I just need to have some fun, Leo. Why does everything always feel so complicated? Why is there always so much happening between people? Why can't it just be – why do I feel I always have to worry about everyone?'

He smiled, genuinely, reassuringly. 'Lovely – you don't have to worry about a single thing. Come here. Big hug! We're fine, believe me. Let's you and me go off to the good ol' US of A and just have a real good time, shall we?'

There it was again, that thing my dad was always saying: the good ol' US of A. It never sounded right coming from my dad, and even less coming from Leo.

'We shall,' I said, trying to ignore the things that were said that didn't sound right, or sounded as if they contained left-over meanings from other conversations. The things that had happened because of Ray's manipulation of me through Leo and Jag still kept making me think that there were ears and eyes everywhere, whispering mouths telling tales, half-truths and distorted facts.

'*Where the bee sucks there suck I,*' Leo sang. '*In a cowslip's bell I lie.*'

I laughed again. 'That's better,' he sang, still tinkling along the keys.

Where the bee stings stung are we,
Lovely Leo and little A-mee!

We laughed and laughed.

'What are we like, eh?' Leo said. 'Come on, let's do some of what we're here to do, shall we?'

'Oh,' I said. 'And what are we here to do, Leo?'

Lovely Leo threw out his hands. 'We're here to entertain, of course,' he said. 'Purely to entertain, my Sweet. As simple as that.'

Love Makes Me Sick

Falling down all over the place
Shaking like a lunatic
A look of madness on my face
Something's making me feel sick.

'No,' Leo said, 'try it more like this.'

And he sang, accompanying himself on the keyboard, in his thin, reedy voice that always entertained while showing a better way of presenting a song every time:

Falling down all over the place
Shaking like a lunatic

But as he sang this time, his voice changed, shifting down in tone as if it faltered. Surely that wasn't what he wanted me to do? It sounded terrible.

'Now you try it,' he said.

I was looking at him, looking to him for more guidance

than this, but Leo was looking down, concentrating on his keys, although this was something he never needed to do.

There was a noise behind me. A door closed. Looking round, there was Ben standing with the Static Cats. The three girls were watching me, but Ben was looking at Leo. Leo glanced up, then down again.

'Hello, Ben,' I said.

Ben smiled at me, briefly. One of his tasks as a runner was to make sure new acts like the Static Cats were where they should be at the right time. The three girls were clinging to him as if their futures depended on it.

'Hello,' I said to the girls.

Ben turned his attention from Leo to me. 'These three gorgeous girls,' he said, 'are the Static Cats.'

'Yes,' I said to them, as they shifted, smiling and blushing, 'I saw you all the other day.'

'We really like what you do,' one of them said.

'Yes,' another stepped forward to say, 'you're like, really doing it.'

'I try,' I smiled.

Leo tried to make his presence felt by playing a little louder, starting to hammer out the tune to *Love Makes Me Sick*. Ben glanced over at him. Leo played a little louder. Ben's face lowered, deepening.

There was some kind of game going on here, some kind of character clash between Leo and Ben. I sometimes think I'm too sensitive, because I can feel situations, my senses acting like antennae, picking up signals of stress and tension. There was so much ill-feeling in the room all of a sudden, so much antagonism running like bad blood between the two of them. Leo disliked having to deal with Ben's instability; it got on his nerves. Ben, sensing Leo's nervousness, was bristling with wary distrust.

'We're rehearsing,' I said to the Cats. 'Come and join us for a while.'

Ben made a great show of looking at his wristwatch.

'Have they got a few minutes, Ben?' I said. 'Come on. Come over here. Listen, this is the song.'

I sang:

Falling down all over the place
Shaking like a lunatic

'You come in here, and here,' I said, showing them my lyric sheet. 'Let's try it.'

Shaking like a lunatic
A look of madness on my face
Something's making me feel sick.

'Yes! Good! Ben, why don't you try getting some drums going for us? Come on, Ben, please.'

Ben stood in his black clothes and lengthening hair like a hip young record producer.

'You can make all this sound so much better, Ben,' I said. 'Can't he, Leo?'

Leo nodded gracefully.

The Static Cats were looking at Ben with such hope, wanting nothing more than to rehearse a song with me, in the Solar studios, as if they were truly part of what happened there. And I wanted nothing more than to dispel this unhealthy atmosphere between Leo and Ben, to clear the air with music.

'Ben?' I said.

The Cats blinked at him. I'm pretty sure one of them purred as Ben handed them copies of the lyric sheets for the song.

'Yes,' I said, as Ben moved to turn on the sound equipment that contained all kinds of synthesizers and drum machines. 'Hear that?' I said, specifically to Ben, as the old background hum of white noise came up to meet Leo as he came tinkling down the scales of his keyboard.

'You know when to come in?' I said to the Cats. They nodded, and then kept on nodding in time to Ben's beat as Leo played the intro to *Love Makes Me Sick*:

Falling down all over the place
Shaking like a lunatic
A look of madness on my face
Something's making me feel sick.

The Cats came in on time, Static Cats moving to the music we were making. Ben looked up. He smiled.

Walking round in a haze
Talking loud and much too quick,
Through restless nights and dog-tired days
You're making me feel lovesick.

The girls and I were dancing, moving around each other, glancing at their lyric sheets as we went, picking up the song incredibly quickly:

But I'd rather feel
So very ill
Than never be in love at all.
Yes, I'd rather feel
So very ill
Than never be in love at all.

They sang beautifully. Ben smiled. These girls actually had

something. They were good. This was the very first time they had heard this song and they were performing it brilliantly, their voices perfectly pitched one against the other:

> *Love makes me sick*
> *But I can't take a pill*
> *Love makes me sick*
> *I must like being ill*
> *Love makes me sick*
> *And it gives me such a thrill.*

They were so good, I'd started to take a back seat by coming in only when they weren't sure where to go next. The four of us sang together:

> *Walking round in a haze*
> *Talking like a lunatic*
> *Through restless nights and dog-tired days*
> *Love's making me feel sick.*

Ben was beaming. Leo was playing – he was just playing, as if this was a rehearsed performance, as if he was happy with the way things were going:

> *But I'd rather feel*
> *So very ill*
> *Than never be in love at all.*
> *Yes, I'd rather feel*
> *So very ill*
> *Than never be in love at all.*

It was as if Leo was happy! As if Ben was! And me! The Static Cats were; they were Ecstatic Cats, pleased to be performing with such a professional team as Leo and Ben and me.

I grinned at Ben, who beamed back.

Love makes me sick
But I can't take a pill
Love makes me sick
I must like being ill
Love makes me sick
And it gives me such a thrill!

Love made us all sick, in one way or another, turning us seasick, green, envious, afraid. Music swept all that away – all of it! For a moment, for a wonderful moment we were –

But the moment could not hold. If only it had, we may have been united, coming together at the end, in the end, as the music died. But the music died. It died and left us too suddenly, as if switched off with Ben's sound equipment, like a silent, malevolent presence at the door.

There *was* a presence standing silent at the door. All eyes turned to him, in his beef-red raw huff.

'That song!' he said.

I felt as if someone should stand up to him, to Ray Ray, the malevolence making itself felt before heard.

'That's new!' he said.

I was expecting Leo to say something.

'We were rehearsing,' I found myself saying, when no other voice but my own came up.

'New song!' Ray insisted, glaring at me, at Ben, fiercest of all at Leo. 'Not for outsiders to hear!' he said. 'Not for outsiders!' Which was placing the Static Cats firmly on the exterior. 'Where they supposed to be?' he asked Ben.

'Studio three,' Ben said.

Ray said nothing.

Ben gathered the dismayed and insulted Cats and led them away. Their experience of Solar: so far so bad, and unlikely to get any better.

'You should know better,' Ray said to Leo.

Leo's curly head twitched, nothing more. He and Ray were eye to eye, but terribly, harmfully.

'Ray,' I said.

'No,' he said, holding up one hand against me. 'No!'

Leo and I watched him walk across the studio and out of the other door. He didn't say anything more; he didn't have to.

He left us there, Leo and I, looking at each other. 'I hate him,' Leo said.

And this time I didn't know what Leo meant: love, or hate.

Twelve

So we were back to square one. No, before that: square nought was where we were, Leo and I, and Ben, Big Ron, the sound technicians, the session musicians. Ray Ray fought the fire of his own fear by fire, dividing to conquer. As soon as any one of us made a move to combine our forces, he would move in mysterious ways to force us back, square one, square nought, re-establishing his power as supreme, as absolute, as always.

Leo and I were still staring at each other when Ben came back in. 'Yeah, thanks,' he said. 'Thanks a lot!' Then he went out again.

Leo and I still hadn't broken eye-contact. 'I've got to get out of here, Lovely,' he said, at length.

'Yes,' I said.

'Are you coming?'

I shook my head. 'I'm going on my own. You go, then I'll go. I'll see you tomorrow, yeah?'

'Yeah,' said Leo, looking the other way.

I ran away for the rest of the day, as simply as that: coat, hat jammed down around my ears. I had done this on the odd occasion in the past, when things like hating Jagdish Mistri, or missing him, or hating and missing him both at once became too much for me to concentrate on what I should have been doing. Leo had done this before, too, for reasons of his own.

I caught a cab home, but stopped the cabbie short as my old school sailed by, the school that Beccs still went to, the one we had intended to leave together to go to university together. I was thinking of the time Beccs and I first became good friends, when I met her at the school I now stood outside. I remembered laughing with her, how I'd suddenly found this other little girl I'd never seen before but laughed with at everything as if we'd been friends forever. That was how it was, that was what it was like with Beccs and me. It was as if we'd always been friends, even before we were friends. As soon as we met we fitted each other, which wasn't to say that we were the same, but we were complementary. With Beccs, I'd always felt more – somehow more easy, complete, as if I was stronger when she was there. She felt the same when she was with me, too. Not that she'd told me, or anything like that; she didn't need to.

Just standing outside the school grounds looking in made me feel better, stronger, more real. I felt nostalgic, kind of teary, but with no tears. Smiles, yes; tears, no. No more tears. Me and Beccs were stronger than that.

The school was practically empty by this time in the afternoon, with only a few groups of boys and girls ambling out of the gates, hanging about in the street laughing, relaxing and having a good time. I supposed, looking at them, that it was this, more than anything that I was missing. I had to hide incognito behind an unusually peaked jockey cap to spy on my old school friends, taking surreptitious photographs to keep on my mobile phone.

I thought I might see Beccs and surprise her, when I saw James Benton, the boy Beccs had told me she had been seeing. Beccs wasn't there. James was with a little man with short hair and a goatee beard as I captured their image on my phone. The man looked a bit scary, but James looked good, with a nice broad smile and good teeth that flashed and then faltered and disappeared as I approached him.

He wandered away from the man and over to a couple of mates of his on the street corner by the school. His nice smile had vanished so completely when he'd noticed me, I thought for a moment he was going to run away. He glanced left and right looking for his best exit route, worried, it seemed, that I was going to be offended because he'd started going out with my best friend.

'Hello, James,' I said.

James's friends fell back from him as I came near. Responding to the look on James's face, they also looked under my cap's peak to determine what was there to worry about so profoundly.

'Hello,' James stammered. 'Hello.'

'Hey!' one of the other boys said. 'Look who it isn't.'

But by now, James had regained his composure. His nice wide smile returned, showing perfectly aligned rows of white teeth. 'Amy,' he said, 'what are you doing here?'

'I only live a few streets away,' I said. 'Was that your dad?'

His smile sparkled. 'Yeah.'

'You still live round here?' the other of James's mates said.

'Course she does,' James laughed. 'Why not?'

'Yeah,' I said to these other boys, the ones who didn't know what on earth to say to me. 'Why not?'

'You took me *so* by surprise,' James turned to me. 'It's like, you know, massively weird, when you see a proper pop star like you just on the street.'

'Yeah,' one of the star-struck boys said. They stammered, James's mates, their familiar faces flushed, searching for more words, failing to find anything further or funnier than 'yeah'.

'I can imagine,' I said.

'What are you doing here? Were you looking for Beccs?'

'Yes. But then I saw you.'

'Well, as it happens I'm just going to see her. She's been on study leave today. Do you want to come and see her with me?'

I smiled at James's smile, pleased for Beccs that she was going out with someone I'd have liked myself. We left the blushing boys kicking their heels before they could decently run off to find people to tell about who they had just seen in the street.

'Is she expecting to see you?' James asked.

A couple of girls I also recognised passed by in the opposite direction without noticing me beneath my low cap. 'Hello, James,' they smiled. All the girls, it seemed, wanted to bask in the sunshine of James's smile.

'Let's surprise her,' I said, as we turned into the street where Beccs lived. 'If she's got her phone on, we'll surprise her. Stand here,' I said, positioning James next to me on Beccs's front doorstep. 'Bend down a bit,' I said, until our heads were level, with the number on Beccs's front door clearly above us in my mobile phone picture-viewer. I captured that image and sent both the images I'd taken of James immediately to Beccs. James and I waited in silence on the doorstep. For minutes, for three or four long silent minutes we smiled and stopped smiling and smiled again, hoping the trick was going to work. Just as we were beginning to think it wouldn't, thunderous footfalls barrelled downstairs on the other side of the door and the door flew open and Beccs flew out.

'I don't believe it!' she cried, kissing us. 'I was like looking at it and looking at it!'

We all fell about laughing. Beccs's mum appeared, wondering what was going on on her own front doorstep. She ushered us all into the hall.

'Look at this!' Beccs said, showing her mum the pictures. 'I was just looking at it and looking at it, thinking, what's going on? I couldn't work it out. James at the school, then the two of them, these two, at our front door!'

We took drinks up to Beccs's room. What a laugh! We couldn't stop. James was like – as if he was one of us. It was nothing at all like being with Ben. Ben soaked up and spoiled our fun, our very sense of fun; but James contributed to it so well that I almost felt as I felt when Beccs and I were alone together against the rest of the world.

'He's so nice,' I hissed to Beccs, when James went out of the room for a while. 'Lovely smile.'

We looked at each other. I can't tell you how much Beccs and I could say to one another in one look like that. Our mutual understanding, our love flashes back and forth until we can't stand it, and we have to collapse in fits again, with tears coming out of our eyes. Just when I had denied myself any more tears, my absolute friend had to reduce me to this, crying with laughter. But these tears were allowed, breathless and sparklingly lovely, alive with joy.

'I can't tell you how much I needed this,' I said.

'And me,' Beccs nodded, indicating the books she had heaped up, spilling over the edges of her computer table.

'I'm really glad you are who you are,' I said.

'I'm glad you are who you are,' she said. 'And,' she said, with that too-close-to-laughter look on her face, 'I'm glad James is who he is.'

I tried not to laugh. We both did. 'I bet you are,' I said, trying to be serious, failing, falling about with Beccs until James came back in and caught us and caught our contagious laughter immediately and made it even madder and wilder and more wonderful.

We just had the most brilliant time. Not once, at any time, did either Beccs or James make any reference to my career or Solar or recording contracts or America or Ben or Car Crime or anything to do with what too often took my life away from this simple laughter, from such a very, very good time. They both quite simply let me off. I couldn't have been more grateful to them. They were beautiful, just right together. It all felt as it should, simple and natural, beyond the grip and grasp of the pop music industry.

It was a holiday, two weeks in a beautiful and relaxing foreign country in two hours in Beccs's untidy bedroom. 'Now I feel ready for America,' I said to Beccs, just after James had gone home.

'Go, girl,' Beccs said. 'Just don't forget who your best friend is when you're living in LA, that's all.'

'I won't forget that,' I said.

I'd never forget that.

✱✱✱ Thirteen

'The good ol' US of A!' my dad kept chanting, next morning. My dad was up for it. 'You up for it, are you?' he kept saying to me, chasing away the holiday feeling from the night before. 'You'll be on the plane tomorrow, well on your way. How do you feel?'

'Mum,' I said, 'I can't help feeling worried about Ben. While we're gone, Leo and me –'

'A-me!' little George said.

'While we're gone, Mum, could you –'

'A-me!' said little Jo.

'The good ol' US of –'

'Have you seen this?' my mum was saying, pointing at what the twins were pointing at in the morning paper.

'A-me!'

'A-me!'

'Harley Davidson!'

'Look. You'd better have a look at this,' she was saying.

'What is it?' my dad said, peering at the upside down pages on the table. 'A picture of Amy Peppercorn in the paper! Well, well. Now there's a thing.'

'No,' my mum said, 'no, listen. Look at what it says.'

We gathered round the newspaper. Jo and George were reading the report out loud. 'Doh-de-dah, de-doh-dah –' it said. Or the twins said it said.

I was reading it myself:

'Doh-de-da – Amy Peppercorn in Brawl Drama – doh-dah-de-dah!'

'What's all this about?' my dad was saying.

'Read it out, Mum,' I said.

'"AMY PEPPERCORN IN BRAWL DRAMA!"' she read. '"New singing sensation Amy Peppercorn was embroiled in a scrap recently, involving her ex-boyfriend and member of Ms Peppercorn's dance group The Car Criminals, and her latest love-interest, the dark and handsome French pop star Adam Bede. The fight –"'

'Fight?' my dad said.

'Fight!' said Jo, trying to punch her sister.

'"The fight,"' my mum continued, '"is reported, by a prominent member of Ms Peppercorn's support team, to have taken place in a recording studio, which was not damaged in any significant way in the affray. Ms Peppercorn is said to have watched her battling suitors with interest and, as reported, some amusement."'

My dad was looking at me. 'Amusement?'

'Ooze-ment,' said George, trying to punch her sister.

My mum looked up. 'Shut up, Tony,' she said, looking down again immediately.

My dad concentrated on separating the fighting girls, looking upon their affray, and the one reported in the paper, with no amusement at all.

My mum read on:

'"A spokesman for Ms Peppercorn's recording company, who also witnessed the scuffle, said, 'Amy sometimes likes to fight fire with fire. She's lovely, really, but sometimes we have difficulty holding her back.' "'

My mum looked up. 'What *is* all this?'

'Oh, no,' I said.

'What's it all about?' my dad said.

But my mum was looking at me, questioning me, demanding an answer.

'It's fighting fire with fire,' I answered, because I was so familiar with that fire-fighting phrase of Leo's, with the desperate fire and firewall of his feeling.

That was the day before Leo and I were due to fly to the States. But that was also the day that the newspapers, as we were to quickly discover, the nastier gutter-rags especially, were awash with all the tall tales.

LITTLE AMY IN BRAWL DRAMA!
AMY – FIGHT FOR ME!
AMY PEPPERCORN IN HOTEL ESCAPADE!

My mum was coming to Solar with me on the morning that the news broke: it sounds so pathetically overblown, news breaking over silly little incidents that might happen in anybody's life. But Amy Peppercorn news broke like a wave blown massively out of all proportion.

It hurt. To have details of my private life brought out and exaggerated in this way, hurt like the fire-on-fire blazes:

AMY PEPPERCORN IN HOTEL ESCAPADE!

Then came this report, hurting, burning to blazes:

In addition to reports of Little Amy Peppercorn's love-interests fighting over her, it has been established that Ms Peppercorn was seen only a couple of months ago departing hurriedly from a hotel in Cornwall, dressed in bed-wear

*from the hotel, and very little else. She is said to have left
the room that she was sharing with a male dancer in a particularly great hurry.*

*The dancer was not involved in the most recent
incident, the brawl at Ms Peppercorn's recording company
studios.*

*Ms Peppercorn's love-interests appear to be quite numer-
ous and very widespread. French superstar Adam Bede is
reported to have had to win Ms Peppercorn's affections by
brute force, encouraged by the diminutive singing sensation
herself.*

*A spokesman for Ms Peppercorn said: 'She's usually so
sweet. She's lovely, really. Sometimes we can't hold her back,
but she's sweet, really. She's lovely.'*

It hurt, to have such things said, followed by, 'she's sweet,
really. She's lovely.' It all sounded so sour, so un-lovely. This
stuff about Jag and Cornwall; how I wanted to forget it. How
could I, when my mum was reading about it, getting details
about the silk pyjama bottoms I'd taken from the hotel when
I'd left it so suddenly.

'It's nothing,' she said, all ready to take on the Solar world
and the whirlwind of the national newspapers.

I felt dizzy. The papers made me sound so – oh, and I
could just imagine how Beccs's cousin Kirsty would be lap-
ping this up! I didn't have to wonder what Courtney
Schaeffer thought. '"Well, I don't know her well enough to
comment," she commented in the press, "but I can't say I'm
surprised."'

How very quickly Courtney could turn around. But maybe
she was being turned around by her managers and by her
press agents. We were both victims of the attitudes and
implications of everything that was written about us. I

couldn't tell what Courtney thought any more than anyone could tell what I was like by reading about me in the papers.

My ears were burning with Solar energy when my mum and I went to the office. Everyone was talking about the newspaper reports. I wanted to talk to Leo about it, about what he'd been saying:

'Amy sometimes likes to fight fire with fire. She's lovely, really, but sometimes we have difficulty holding her back.'

It sounded like the fire fighting he'd been doing lately, but I couldn't believe he'd told them everything else, all those details I felt so embarrassed about watching my mum read.

'We'll find out what's been going on,' she said, going up to Ray's office. She wanted me to go with her, but I wanted to find Leo. I found Ben.

He gave me a look very much like the one he'd left me with yesterday in the studio.

'Ben,' I said, 'has this newspaper stuff got anything to do with you?'

He looked again. His face appeared disgusted enough for me to believe him: 'I'm not the one who's been talking to Barry Bone,' he said. 'Not me. I'm just a runner. Leo's the spokesman, not me.'

'Where is he?'

'Leo? I don't know.'

'Haven't you seen him?'

'No. Nobody has.'

'Who's Barry Bone, anyway?'

Ben smiled. 'Don't you know? You don't know anything, do you.'

He was right, of course. It was what I'd been saying to Leo

yesterday: I didn't know enough – I didn't understand enough. I just didn't get it.'

'Who's Barry Bone?' I said again.

'He's a reporter,' Ben said.

'Oh,' I said.

'Yeah. And he's on your case.'

'What do you mean, on my case?'

'That's what Barry Bone does. Haven't you seen his stuff in the papers? Celebrity dirt. Barry Bone, dirt digger. And he's well on to you, Amy.'

'And that makes you glad, does it?'

Ben shrugged. 'Not my dirt,' he said. 'Nothing to do with me, is it?' He looked as if he felt better all of a sudden. I wondered what kind of wild, speed-driven obsession would inspire Ben to feel better next time, or the time after that, or the time after that. Now I knew that Ben could never just feel good. He felt bad, or else madly inspired. Nothing in between. That was what the smoking and the drinking were about. He wasn't happy with himself, but couldn't express his unhappiness or live with it without trying to force unhappiness on others.

'Where's Leo?' I said.

'Okay?' Ray asked my mum, ignoring me.

My mum kept glancing at me.

'Where's Leo?'

'We don't know,' my mum said.

'You can go to America?' Ray asked. 'Such short notice?'

'Yes. The school have already found a replacement for –'

'But what about Leo?' I said.

'Leo's out,' Ray said.

'Out?'

'Out,' he restated, as if that was it, all there was to say on the matter. 'Out!'

'But you don't know even if it was him!' I said, meaning the report in the papers.

'Amy,' my mum said, coming over to me, 'Leo's got some sorting out to do here. He'll be all right.'

'Will he?' I asked, doubtfully. 'If he's being blamed for those newspaper stories – '

'Blamed?' Ray said. 'No blame. No problem.'

'No problem?'

'Forget it. You're in the papers, you're in the papers. Better than not being in the papers.'

'It's okay, Amy,' my mum said. 'We can go together, you and I. It'll work out. Leo's just got some sorting out to do –'

Nobody told me what sort of "sorting out" Leo had to do. I didn't see him, couldn't get through to him, so had no chance of finding out how he was. My mum was coming with me to America; I'd wanted that, only now it felt strange, going without Leo.

'The good ol' US of –'

'A!' Jo and George cried.

'US of A!' my dad yelped, when my mum told him she was going after all. He'd never been to the States, but talked about it as if he knew every bit of it intimately. 'The Big Apple!' he said. 'Harley Davidson!'

'McDonald's,' my mum said, trying to bring him back down to earth.

'Big Mackie D!' he exclaimed.

The girls clapped their hands. We were all in the kitchen

discussing the trip. My mum was excited, but trying not to show it. My dad was showing enough excitement for us all.

'LA!' he barked.

'We shan't be going anywhere near there,' my mum laughed.

'No,' he said. 'But still.'

But still I felt uneasy about Leo and about the horrible things Barry Bone had written about me in his nasty little newspaper. It all felt very strange, somehow related to the friction between Leo and Ben – almost as if Ray Ray had engineered all this to divide and conquer us again, using jealousy and suspicion, even inspiring negative newspaper reports, which, he said, were 'no problem'. Better that than not being in the papers at all: that was Ray's philosophy. Bad news was better than no news at all, according to Ray.

'Still,' my dad said, 'the City of Angels! Central Park! Park Lane!'

'Park Lane's in London, Tony,' my mum laughed.

'Oh yeah,' said my dad. 'Still.'

⁎⁎ Fourteen

Leo had disappeared. The idea of Raymond killing him and hiding his body occurred to me more than once, more than twice, becoming less and less of a joke every time I thought about it.

'Don't be silly,' Beccs told me, over the phone, that evening.

I wanted to see her again, before my flight, but she was out with James. She sent me a snapshot of James bowling.

It wasn't that I actually thought that Ray had killed Leo. It was just a silly worry, brought on by all the fuss and bother that had suddenly broken into and increased the madness of my mad pop star life.

'That's just silly,' Beccs said. 'He's just lying low for a while.'

'You don't know what this will do to him,' I said. 'He's out. Ray's kicking him out. Leo won't be able to take it.'

'People cope,' Beccs said. 'James says hello, by the way. I've got to go, Amy,' she said. 'It's my turn to bowl. I'll call you later. We can talk properly.'

I took a snapshot of myself smiling, for Beccs to show James. But as soon as the picture had been taken, my smile slipped and I was waving to no one. My mum was coming to America with me, as my guide and chaperone. My mum! I was a pop star! As much as I wanted her there, on my side, as much as I needed to confide in her, I couldn't help feeling slightly ridiculous going on a mini radio and TV tour of New York and Philadelphia with my mother. The papers were making me out to be some kind of a boy-crazy spoilt brat. So my mum had decided not to let me out of her sight, or so it might seem. How quickly those dismal, sensation-seeking, sunny, funny, punny, grubby little dailies turned against the very people they helped set up in the first place.

It wasn't Leo's fault, even if he had been speaking to Barry Bone. What was Leo, what had he always been, but an unstoppable chatterbox and gossip? I was sure he'd never meant to harm anyone. I hoped he'd never mean any harm to himself.

We were off to America, my mum and I, but I felt as if the walls were tumbling here, the foundations crumbling. Ray might have been happy with any kind of publicity; it was me that had to live with what they said.

My mum was great about it all, though. 'It doesn't alter the truth about you,' was all she said. She was good for me. She made me go up to bed early. I wasn't sleeping. Neither was she, I knew. The twins slept, so did my dad. He had worn himself out by infuriating himself all day over the newspaper reports, then exciting himself about America all over again. My dad, the most harmless person in the world, was lovely and totally ineffective. My mum must have been as worried about the papers as I was, but she was also just as excited about America as my dad, sitting up in bed reading by the light on her side of the bed while he snored and snuffled and dreamed of Harley Davidsons in the good ol' US of A.

A picture-text came through. Beccs had snapped a shot of James kissing her at the bowling alley. I could have cried. Could have, but didn't. Beccs was with me. She wanted me with her.

She called. 'Did you get my picture?'

'Yes. What's it like, kissing him?'

We laughed. That's what we did.

'Oh,' she said, 'so nice.'

'I never asked you, how did you two get together?'

Beccs laughed. 'Playing football.'

I laughed, too. 'That's ideal. Football sweethearts.'

We laughed again. We always laughed, even when we felt like crying. But the laughter always seemed to originate from Beccs, these days. She started it, she kept it going. I was forever being far too serious. I don't know what I would have done without her.

'I'm worried about Leo,' I said.

'I know,' she said.

'He didn't mean to do anything to me.'

'Maybe not,' she said. 'But Ben said – '

'Ben?'

'Ben said that that paper pays people a lot of money for stories about people like you.'

'You've been speaking to Ben?'

'Yes. He seems – better. He's quite enthusiastic.'

'Yes,' I said, 'enthusiastic when it comes to showing attitude. That's what Ben's got to do to feel better. It's not right, none of it!'

'But you're the one the papers are on at. Did you see that bit that Courtney said about you?'

'None of it's true,' I said.

'No,' Beccs said, 'but how can anybody be sure what the truth really is?'

'I don't know,' I said. 'I really do not know.'

And if I didn't know, who did?

'Anyway,' Beccs said, 'you're off to America tomorrow.'

'Yeah, with my mum.'

'That's good, isn't it?'

'Yeah. But I'll be out with my mum the whole time. Would you like to spend more than a whole week with your mum?'

She laughed. 'We'd drive each other up the wall. We do now. But my mum's not like your mum, is she? Your mum's like, you know. You'll have a lot of fun together, you're bound to.'

'I hope you're right. It'll be an experience anyway, for us both.'

'New York, eh? You have to go to Manhattan, Brooklyn, the Bronx, everywhere.'

'Everywhere? New York's a big place, you know.'

'Yeah, I know. And it's a long way away. When you come back, all this nonsense in the papers will be forgotten about.'

'I do hope so,' I said.

'It will. And Leo'll be back and Ben'll be fine and you'll see you've been worrying about nothing again.'

'Yes, again,' I said. 'I'm always worrying about nothing.'

'So don't!' she said.

'Don't go away, though,' I said.

'Don't start worrying about me,' she laughed. 'The one thing you don't have to worry about, is me.'

That was Beccs. I went to sleep shortly after that, thinking about the one thing I didn't have to worry about: my best friend.

Fifteen

It felt just like a holiday, going away with my mum like that. When my dad and the twins waved us off as we disappeared through the gate at Heathrow, it was just as if we were escaping, just the two of us, for an American vacation.

'Do you know,' my mum said, as we were waiting in line to have our passports and boarding cards checked, 'I feel I deserve this holiday.'

I laughed. 'And do you know,' I said, 'you must have been reading my mind.'

'Yes,' she smiled, 'I was.'

I believed her, too. Sometimes it was like that, with my mum. How often in the past had she looked into me, seeing through my painted expression to the root of what was bothering me. 'I'm glad we're going together,' I said.

'So am I,' she said. 'And Leo's fine. Ray told me. It's a personal thing, between the two of them. Leo couldn't leave it, not right now.'

'Then it's nothing to do with the newspaper reports?' I said.

She shook her head as the passport control officer looked at us then looked at me again. He waved us on with just a flicker of recognition in my direction.

'Are you sure, Mum?' I said, as we waited in the next queue to go through the metal-detector and for our hand luggage to pass through the X-ray machine. 'Are you sure Leo's all right?'

'Yes I am,' she said. 'Ray told me.'

That, of course, failed to convince me.

'Look,' she said, X-raying through to my doubts and worries, 'Ray talked to me yesterday morning about his relationship with Leo. Do you know how difficult it is for a man like Ray to do that? He assured me, it's personal. Between the two of them. You'll have to trust my judgement on this one, Amy.'

'Yes, Mum,' I said, because I trusted my mum's judgement better than anyone's; certainly better than I trusted Ray's assurances.

'I mean it,' she said.

'So do I,' I said.

'Then we can stop worrying?'

'We can stop worrying.'

'Good. Don't let me forget to stop off in duty-free on the way home. I told your dad I'd get him a bottle of something very expensive. He thinks it'll be whisky. It'll be aftershave. I prefer the smell.'

The cabin crew were handing out newspapers as we boarded the plane. 'No thanks,' my mum said before I could reach to take one.

'Let's just stick to our magazines and books, shall we?' she said as we made our way to our seats.

'Yes,' I said, 'let's.' We were leaving all that behind, sitting strapping ourselves in with seatbelts, turning on the airvents above our heads, checking out the in-flight magazine: I wasn't in it.

My mum smiled at me as I scanned the pages. 'It's a holiday,' she said, almost whispering, as if it was a secret we shared.

I put the magazine away and hugged her. 'We're flying away,' I whispered, 'for a holiday.'

'Right away,' she said, 'thousands and thousands of miles. Thousands and thousands.'

'You were miles away,' she said.

I was trying to get a decent stretch. 'So were you,' I said. 'I woke up earlier and you were fast asleep.'

'Only for a while, though,' she said. 'I couldn't get to sleep last night.'

'No, neither could I.'

'I kept thinking of New York and Philadelphia.'

'So did I,' I said, although I was thinking about how much Leo had been looking forward to going there and how disappointed he'd be to miss out.

'We'll be landing soon,' my mum said.

'Good,' I said.

'Imagine,' she said, 'all that ocean, the Atlantic, between England and America, and we're almost on the other side of it.'

'And my shoulders feel like I've swum most of the way,' I said, still trying to stretch.

Queuing again at passport control, waiting at the baggage reclaim conveyor, the Atlantic Ocean didn't seem all that wide at all. In fact, from one airport to another, from one queue to the next, it seemed like no distance. Signs welcomed us to America, but so far it still felt like Heathrow, England.

Then Ray Ray's American promoter met us in Arrivals and the yellow cabs were lined up outside and the air felt different and the background sounds were not English and we were in America.

'Hey!' Al Gerard III bellowed at us. 'Hey! Hey! Hey! Amy Peppercorn and Mrs Amy Peppercorn!'

'It's Jill, actually,' my mum smiled, with a glance at me.

'Jill!' Al grinned, shaking my mum's hand, then mine. 'Welcome to the US. Ray told me you were bringing your mom,' he said to me.

'That's okay, isn't it?' I said.

'Okay?' Al Gerard III whooped, in a desert storm of tumbleweed enthusiasm. 'Okay? Wow! It's the best. I mean, yeah. I like it, the guys like it when someone brings their mom.'

'Well,' I said, 'she's bringing me, really.'

'Cool!' Al said. 'Cool! The guys are so looking forward to meeting you guys. Everybody's bigged, yeah?'

We were wheeling our baggage trolley out to the car park.

'We'll have a little time to rest, though,' my mum said, 'won't we?'

'Oh, sure,' said Al. 'We don't want our young star jet-lagged, do we now. Sure. Rest up, rest of today, tonight. Tomorrow, meet the guys, do the first radio interview. City station. Practically on our doorstep. No problem, Amy?'

'No problem,' I said.

'Cool you brought your mom, though,' Al laughed. 'That

other British girl we had over, she brought her mom, too. Courtney?'

'Courtney Schaeffer?' I said.

'Yeah,' he said, as we clambered into his very new, very sparkly automobile. 'No,' he said, 'no, my mistake. Pardon me. Charlotte, she brought her mom. Courtney came on her own. I remember now, Courtney came on her own.'

Sixteen

'Mum?' I had my lips close to the frame of her door. We had adjacent rooms in a very big and sumptuous hotel. I'd left my door open behind me. 'Mum?' I tapped gently, thinking she might be asleep.

'Why aren't you asleep?' she asked, opening her door to me, standing in the corridor.

'I can't,' I said. 'I'm not tired.'

'You must be.'

'Well why aren't you asleep then?' I said.

It was still early afternoon there and the sun was out playing in the street.

'New York's right outside,' I said, jumping up and down. 'I can't sleep, can I? How can I sleep?'

'You'll be tired tonight.'

'I'll sleep well tonight. Mum, come on. New York! Let's go! I'm just bursting to see some of it. Let's get a coffee in one of those places in Manhattan you see on TV. Let's go shopping! Let's –'

'Okay! Okay!' she laughed. 'Let's get a cab. I've always wanted to ride uptown in a yellow cab. That's what they say, isn't it: uptown?'

'That's what they say, Mum. Uptown. Let's take a cab ride uptown.'

***

Oh, we went uptown and down again, left and right, jumping in and out of cabs, looking, pointing, seeing the sights. Being in NYC, the Big Apple, with my mum, was great. It was really great. Manhattan's an island. I never knew that. It was beautiful. We had coffee with cream and chocolate, coffee chocolate and cream. We were licking our lips like a couple of cats. It was so strange, seeing my mum like this. She was – she was a friend, a real good friend. I kept thinking how great it would be to come back to New York with Beccs one day, but my mum was a funny, lovely friend and I felt safe with her. She made me laugh again and again. If Beccs had been there with us, the three of us would have been a riot.

I'd never been away with just my mum before. It wasn't at all as I'd been expecting. We were both tired I suppose, which somehow only helped us to relax. We just had a good time, eating and drinking, laughing, shopping, trying on clothes. I was out with a mate. You should have seen some of the stuff I got my mum to try on. My dad would have burst a blood vessel. She tried on more clothes than I did! Which wasn't surprising, really, when you considered all the things designers and retailers were always sending to me through Solar. All I did sometimes was try on clothes back home. So it was my mum's turn. Little black dresses! Really nice trousers! Lovely tops and blouses!

She didn't buy anything outrageous, of course. We were just messing. But she did buy some beautiful tops and a lovely pair of trousers that I would have worn, and two pairs of shoes and a skirt that, while it wasn't exactly short, was a whole lot higher than anything I'd ever seen her wearing. 'Your dad'll like this,' she said, looking at her reflection in the full-length mirror. The shop we were in was the stuff fantasies were made of. It was sheer uptown NYC, and so was my mum, for that moment. I couldn't believe how good she looked.

'Do I look ridiculous?' she asked.

'You look fantastic,' I said. 'Just fantastic.'

'Well,' she said, 'I want to look my best for the radio and television companies. I am Amy Peppercorn's mum, after all.'

'Yes,' I said. 'Yes you are.'

There was no point in returning to the hotel too early that evening; although we were both worn out, my mum and I knew we were too wound up and excited to go to sleep. New York at night was something we just had to experience together. Some of the bridges across the river were so pretty. The lights were just unbelievable. There were so many restaurants to choose from for dinner, we tried to ask a yellow cab driver to take us to the best one he knew that would let us in without a booking; but his English was so bad, he couldn't understand what we were talking about. He was Puerto Rican, my mum thought. We had to change cabs and try again.

The place we were taken to was so big and brash and loud I thought my mum would hate it. She loved it. It was almost as if I was just finding out about her. It's easy to miss so much about a person when you're always so close to them. Your mum's just your mum, right? But away together on a night out in this new and sparkling city, I was able to see her in a different light, against a different background.

'Isn't it great here?' she said, looking round at the busy restaurant.

'Isn't everything great here?' I said.

'I've never been this far from home before,' she said. 'Greece, I suppose, is the furthest I've been. The funny thing

108

is, all this way, and I don't feel far from home at all. Do you?'

'No,' I agreed, 'I don't. I've got my mum with me, haven't I.'

'Yes,' she said. 'And you were wrong about what you said to Al Gerard.'

'What did I say?'

'When you said I'd brought you. That was wrong. You've brought me. I wouldn't be here if you hadn't done all you've done.' She looked around again. Her eyes were sparkling. 'It's fantastic,' she said.

'Yes,' I said, looked at our surroundings, appreciating it all with her.

'No,' she said, 'not just all this. I mean what you've done. It's wonderful. I don't know if I've ever told you how proud I am of you.'

'Mum!' I laughed. 'You'll have me in tears if you carry on.'

'No,' she said, 'no. People point me out in the street at home, almost as if I was famous too.'

I laughed again. 'Do they?'

'They do. I know what they're saying. They're saying, Look, there's Amy Peppercorn's mum. I'm always pretending I haven't noticed or it means nothing to me; but it does. It's like –' she said, as the waiter came up to take our order and my mum went for a cheeseburger with fries and onion rings as if she ate stuff like that every day without ever having gone on and on about how bad it was for me.

'But I thought – ' I started to say.

She waved me down. 'Yeah, yeah, yeah,' she said. 'Whatever!'

We laughed and laughed.

***

Back at the hotel, I was supposed to be getting ready for bed. Cleaning my teeth, rinsing my face, I kept remembering all the things we'd done that afternoon and evening, my mum and I. It was all so very good. I still felt excited and about a million miles away from sleep. I wanted to do what I always did whenever anything exciting happened: speak to Beccs and tell her all about it. There was a telephone tempting me on the table in my room. My mum had made me promise to go straight to bed, as we were so very late back. But it would still be late afternoon, or very early evening in England and Beccs would be home from school and waiting for my call. My excitement felt like Beccs's excitement, as if it was part of the same thing. That's how close we were. I'd burst if I didn't share it with her soon.

My mum and I wouldn't have to pay the bill for the hotel; that would be taken care of by Al Gerard III. But we'd be charged for any extras, like telephone calls, so my mum would find out I'd been chatting to Beccs late at night when I should have been sleeping. But I wouldn't sleep if I didn't speak to her, so I went down to the hotel lobby to use the public phones there. Waiting for change at reception, I glanced down the newspaper rack, not exactly looking for the English papers, but not exactly not looking for them. If they were there, they were there.

They were there, all of them. I supposed I shouldn't have picked that one up, picking out the very rag that Barry Bone wrote for, collecting my change, thumbing through the pages while I waited to be put through to the UK.

The phone rang for a long while, giving me far, far too much time to read:

GLOBE-TROTTING AMY RETREATS TO US!

I had to go on reading, as Beccs wasn't answering:

Proud singing star, Amy Peppercorn, who is currently attempting, like so many before her, to break into the lucrative American pop-music market, is reported to have been 'really glad to get away' and leave what's left of her tangled love-life in disarray. With one love-interest in France, one a dancer in a West-End show, one a young record producer, Ms Peppercorn seems to be a –

'Hello?' a voice said, abruptly.
'Hello?'
'Is that Amy?' It was Beccs's mum.
'Yes, Mrs Bradley, it's me. Is – '
'Amy,' she said.
My eye was being drawn back to the printed page:

Ms Peppercorn seems to be a very –

'Amy,' Mrs Bradley said, 'do you know what time it is?'
'Here, it's – '
'No,' she interrupted, shortly. 'Here. It's the early hours of the morning. What are you doing phoning at this hour?'
'Oh,' I said.

Ms Peppercorn seems to be a very confused –

'Oh, indeed,' Mrs Bradley snapped. 'Amy, I can only think you've got yourself very confused.'

– a very confused and self-centred young lady.

'Mrs Bradley,' I said, 'I'm so sorry. I'm too self-centred sometimes – '

'No,' she said, softening, 'not at all. It's all right. These things happen. I'll tell Rebecca you called. In the morning, if that's all right with you?'

'Of course. Sorry I disturbed you.'

'Don't mention it, Amy. You're just confused, at the moment.'

'Yes,' I said. 'I'm just confused.'

*** Seventeen

I was confused. Al Gerard III collected us next day to meet 'the guys', who turned out to be practically all girls. But it was sleep, dream-broken sleep that was confusing me more than the girl-and-guy guys in Al's office. Last night I had tossed that newspaper away in the lobby before going back to my room to bed. How I had confused the time difference between New York and England, I didn't know. But I had, which proved Barry Bone and his horrible little paper correct: confused I was.

Last night the sun still seemed to be up outside my room. There was so much light out on the street night never seemed to come; I felt as if I'd waited a long, long time for it to happen, then it didn't happen. Usually I slept well all night – usually I wasn't this confused, mistaking one time of the day for another, wondering how high the sun was in various particular places in the world, confirming my confusion in yesterday's English newspapers.

An aeroplane buzzed through my dreams as I floated along some way above deep sleep. Waking, engines of air-con thrummed as if threatening from a near horizon. The glow from outside was like a deep orange sunset on a cheap postcard. The bottled water from the mini-bar in my room was chilled almost to ice. Something in the burger I'd eaten, some salt gherkin, was dehydrating me, driving me to drink, to swill cold, cold water until my right eye was aching. Back in bed, only to find I needed the loo. Then the air-con ground louder, or seemed to, as I grew more tired but no more sleepy. I had to drink some more. I had to go to the loo again. I had another dream that wasn't quite a dream, more like a montage of images from my immediate surroundings. They were too immediate, these surroundings of mine, confusing me still further with day that was night, aeroplane engines without flight, thirst, cold water, clammy sheets.

The 'guys' were lovely girls and very up, and so were we, my mum and me. Me and Mum. I had to admit to her that I hadn't slept well, because she could see the effect on me. I could see her glances in my direction, with a slight nag of worry in her brow. 'Have you taken your medication?' she said.

'I didn't get any deep sleep last night,' I said, without saying anything about that telephone call, my mistakes with time and newspapers. 'But I'm fine,' I said. 'I feel good.'

I did feel good – much better than I was expecting. We were still on holiday. This was going to be great. We were going to have fun, if it killed me.

It wouldn't kill me. I smiled. We were strong together, Mum and I. Not quite as strong though as the mountain of a man towering over us suddenly, blocking most of the light from the window in Al's office.

'Guys,' Al said, 'this is Franklin – Frank. He's your driver, while you're in New York. Cars will pick you up in Philadelphia, at the airport, yeah?'

My mum stood up to shake hands with Frank. Her hand looked tiny against his. In it, her hand just disappeared. 'Pleased to meet you, Frank,' she said.

'Pleasure's all mine,' he said. He was dressed in black: not music business black, with jeans and shirt and jacket, but bouncer black, with combats tucked into high boots, a plump bomber-jacket adding to the critical mass of his body.

'Are we ever going to feel safe in this city,' my mum said, turning to me, 'or what?'

She made me laugh again and again. If ever I had had any doubts at all about being chaperoned by my mother, they had evaporated, freeze dried and been blown away by my mum's cool.

Late morning, and we were due to leave Al's office for lunch before riding behind our shotgun driver to the first radio station. The tour was to be mostly radio, with one NY television appearance at the end.

'I need to call Beccs before we leave,' I said to my mum. I'd worked out the times correctly by now, calculating when Beccs would be home from school but not yet out with James Benton. It made me feel strange, working out what time it was at home while keeping a proper hold on what time it was there in America. I don't wear a watch, but usually have this kind of innate awareness of how early or late it is, by how hungry I am, how tired, and all kinds of other internal and external clues. But nothing felt the same somehow. The flavour of that gherkin or whatever it was I'd eaten last night kept repeating on me, spoiling my appetite for breakfast and lunch. That must have been some rock-solid pickle, sticking to my ribs, still dehydrating me throughout the morning.

'Is it a good time to call home?' my mum laughed. 'I haven't got a clue what time it is there.'

We called my dad together before I called Beccs:

'How's it going?' he shouted. The line was perfect. If he'd

115

whispered we would have heard him. 'How are the inter-views going?'

'We haven't done any yet,' I said.

'Give me the phone,' my mum said. 'Tony, it's me. Yes. How are the twins? Yes – no, we, ah, haven't seen them. It doesn't matter. No.' She listened for a long time, glancing at me now and then, smiling on and off. 'Okay,' she said, 'we will. Good. Say hello and goodbye to the twins for me. Amy wants to say goodbye.'

He'd been telling her about something, I could tell, by the way my mum had been glancing at me. When I said good-bye to my dad, his voice told me he'd been telling my mum something, something to do with me. His voice told me that, he didn't.

'What are you like?'

'I know,' I said. 'I'd forgotten which way the clocks went; don't ask me how. Tell your mum I'm sorry I woke her up.'

'Oh, she's all right. She thought it was funny when she was telling me about it this morning. How's New York?'

'Beccs, it's fantastic!'

'I knew you'd think so.'

'Yeah, but it is. So cool. And my mum! She's like a differ-ent person here. It's like seeing another side to her I've never seen before.'

'I'll have to go with my mum,' she laughed.

'You'll have to go with me! One time, you and me, here. We'd have a fantastic time. We'd love it! We'd have so much fun. We're just off to the first radio station.'

'Your first American broadcast! Good luck!'

'Thanks. I hope we won't need any luck.'

'I'm sure you won't. Good luck, anyway. What's it called, this first radio station?'

'Oh – do you know, I can't even remember. Can you believe it? Bad, isn't it? My head's all over the place.'

'You're confused,' Beccs said.

'Yeah,' I said, 'but we're driving all over the city and the provinces, after today. Then flying to Philadelphia – anyway, how are things back there?'

'Oh, you know, same as ever.'

'And,' I said, trying, but failing to stop myself from asking, 'what about the papers? Still on about me?'

She laughed. 'Forget about it,' she said. 'It's all rubbish.'

'Yeah, I know. What are they saying?'

'Oh, nothing, you know. Some rubbish.'

'Yeah. What rubbish?'

She sighed. 'Something about – drugs? On tour? You know, Leo, Jag, downers and uppers –'

'Does it say that?'

'No, not really. Look, it's nothing.'

'That Barry Bone!'

'Who?'

'The newspaper reporter. Barry Bone.'

'Look,' Beccs said, 'don't worry about it. It's all a load of –'

But they were knocking on the door for me. 'Beccs, I have to go.'

'Yes,' she said, 'go. Don't worry. Do your radio shows. Have a great time. You'll be fine. You'll be fine.'

Twice, she said it: you'll be fine. You'll be fine.

And I was, fine: doubly fine. The first radio interview in New York was such fun, I couldn't stop talking about myself, my family, my friends. They wanted to know everything. My mum was in an adjoining room with glass walls, giving me the thumbs-up and grinning at me. She had headphones on, listening, laughing, loving it with me. The DJ was called Toby Blue, to "chase away the blues". He knew my songs. He'd been playing *If Ever* and *Proud* on his show for the past week.

Toby asked me, on air, about my first public performance of *If Ever*. I told Toby and his radio audience all about Geoff Fryer, and how I'd been thinking of him when I'd first done that song. It felt right, talking about it like that. It felt as if the old wounds were finally healing at last.

'You know what I'm really looking forward to?' asked my mum that evening, as we dined in the hotel restaurant on 'proper food', as she put it, fish and salad and fruit.

'A good night's sleep?' I said.

'Yes,' she said, 'that; and I'm looking forward to being recognised on the streets of New York, people pointing me out, going, Look, there's Amy Peppercorn's mum.'

I laughed.

'Because if all the interviews go as well as this one,' she said, 'it's not going to take long. You'll make it here. It's right. I can feel it.'

'I hope you're right,' I laughed.

She laughed too. 'I am. But you're right about that good night's sleep,' she said.

Eighteen

This was supposed to have been the good night's sleep I needed to prepare myself for the car journeys and the interviews to come. As it was, the newspaper I shouldn't have read I re-read again and again in my head, agitating my mind with images of Barry Bone 'on my case'. Somehow he had got to Leo when Leo was at a low ebb, exploiting his emotions – well, I had to sympathise with Leo there. In fact, I sympathised with him everywhere, on everything. I wanted to see him, or at least talk to him.

It's never any use, *trying* to sleep. Trying for it made sleep slip further and further from my mind. For a moment I tried to work out what time it was at home, but abandoned the attempt almost immediately as I didn't even know what time it was in my hotel room. But whatever the time, or my mum's disapproval, I was going to call Leo straight away. I needed him. He needed me. I could feel he needed me, almost as if it was he keeping me from sleep. We needed each other. If we could talk, we'd sleep, both of us: because I knew he wasn't sleeping. And knowing that was keeping me awake.

'You should have been sleeping,' my mum said, as I'd expected, about my call to Leo.

'Leo' I had said into his answering machine, 'I'm thinking of you. New York's fabulous. You'd love it. I'm just surprised you've never been.'

He'd never been there, or anywhere else in America. Leo would have been at home in New York, I felt, when I thought about him from there. Leo would have come back to life in that city, far enough away from Ray Ray's solar ray-gun.

'Leo's fine,' my mum said, trying to read my mind. 'He's fine. Stop worrying. Relax. Concentrate on what you're doing here. Honestly, you're a bigger worrier than I am sometimes.'

The DJ, Wolfe McVitie, laughed. 'No way!' he laughed. 'You brought your mom!'

'Well,' I said, 'she brought me, actually.'

'No way!' he bellowed over the airwaves. 'Hey! D'you hear this? Amy – Peppercorn? Is it Peppercorn? . . . Great name! Amy Peppercorn's here. She's a big R&B star in – no? She's a big star anyways, over the pond there in the small isle of old England, an' she's brought her mom with her on tour in the US. Hey, is that a gas, or is that a gas? Where's your mom now, Amy?'

'She's just out there. There she is, with the headphones on.'

'Really? That's your mom?'

My mum was shaking her head and holding up her hands, almost as if to deny that she was my mum.

'Cool,' Wolfe said. 'Bring her in. Let's bring her on – can somebody fetch Amy's mom? We'll play the song, eh? The song's called – Amy?'

'The song's called *Proud*, from my album, also called *Proud*.'

'This song's called *Proud*, people. Here's proud Amy, on her way, in the good ol' US of A!'

'Let's go out.'

'Do you really think that's a good idea?'

'Why not?'

'Where to? We're in a very different part of the city, don't forget. We don't know what it might be like.'

'Come on: a restaurant at least. One of those lively places like the one we were in the other night.'

'We've got another early one tomorrow, don't forget.'

'What do we sound like?' my mum laughed. 'We've mixed up roles somewhere along the way, haven't we?'

'Yeah,' I said, 'in that radio station, I think.'

'I think so too,' she said. Her eyes were sparking; and I do mean sparks were coming out of them. We were being driven to the hotel. My mum had been sparking ever since we'd both done the last but one radio interview. So funny! We were a great double act, the pop star and her ex-maths teacher mother. I was booked to be on air for fifteen minutes: we were on for over half an hour.

My mum was flying. I couldn't stop laughing. She wanted to go out, of all things, while I thought it best we had a quiet night at the hotel.

'You're right,' she said. 'We'll go to bed nice and early.'

'No,' I said, 'you're right. It's too early. There's no point. I'll not sleep if I go to bed too early. Let's go somewhere.'

'Somewhere lively,' she said, with all that excitement still sparking from her.

My mum was always looking out of the window as we were driven from one radio station to another, at a series of dashing, disparate light shows flitting by. I couldn't look at it any more.

'Are you all right, Amy? How are you feeling?'

'Tired.'

'We'll be at the hotel soon. We'll have a bath and some dinner straight away and get to bed.'

Since the moment the plane had powered up to bring us here, the engines hadn't stopped, not for an instant. My mum was proving to be much better at this than I was. She was cool; that is, her temperature didn't fluctuate like mine, flushing my cheeks red.

'Are you all right?' she kept asking. 'Have you taken your medication? Would you like something else to drink?'

My mouth had that kind of nervous thirst I always got just before an interview. This was the way I felt before every interview, but America had somehow started making me feel this way all the time.

We called my dad. 'How's it going over there?' he bellowed down the telephone line, trying to shout all the way here unassisted.

'Good,' my mum said. 'Good.'

'How's Ames?'

'She's fine.'

'And how are the interviews going?'

'Oh, fine. They're fine.'

'Good reports back, so far,' my dad shouted. 'Solar are in touch all the way.'

Yes, I thought, the sun never sets on the Solar system. Ray Ray chased us round the radio stations, plotting our progress by phone as I waited in traffic behind our driver, Franklin, trying desperately not to feel car sick.

✳✳✳ Nineteen

I had no idea of the time or what day it was. Four New York nights had passed, and it was night, or early morning. Last night we had flown to Philadelphia. But the nights were the same, this hotel room a clone of the last. The digits on my mobile said – my phone wasn't even switched on. I'd lost track of time, and the telephone line somewhere on the first flight across the Atlantic to the Home of the Free.

That was my dad again. The Home of the Free, he kept calling it. America. The good ol' etc, etc. My dad had this image of freeways that weren't like motorways, but open roads across deserts with snowy mountain ranges off in the distance. He had this dream of a sit-back motorbike-ride in jeans and leather jacket across a magnificent landscape towards a high-rise haven city sparkling on the horizon.

I had an image through my headache of crowded streets, yellow cabs and yelling drivers, a grinding chorus of extractor fans and false dirty street lighting. This uncomfortably huge land, the big business enterprise of it, I was beginning to feel, couldn't possible be interested in Little Amy P. There was too much here, too much going on already to make room for me, surely, wasn't there?

'You're very quiet,' my mum said, as streetlamps approached and slid away behind us on our latest ride. Dirty rain started to fall. The anonymous driver up front flicked on the window wipers.

'Are you sure you're okay, Amy?'

'Yes,' I said. 'I've got a headache.'

'You've taken your medication, haven't you?'

'Yes, I told you. Of course I have. Mum, I'm not going to have a seizure. I'm just tired.'

'So am I,' she said. The sparks had stopped flying out of her eyes days ago. We needed them, but our batteries were running down. 'This is hard work.'

'Tell me about it,' I said. And I hated it when people said that. But I said it, even though the last thing I wanted was for my mum to start telling me.

'This is too much for you,' she told me. 'The fun's going out of it.'

'This next DJ's called Horse,' I said. 'That should be fun.'

'Let's hope so,' she said.

I really did hope so, because for the last couple of days I'd felt I hadn't been able to say or do anything to impress anybody. The truth was, I was never very good at interviews: I communicated best with an audience when I was – I suppose when I was something much bigger and better than the little me I'd so far presented to the Americans. All I felt I'd done was stammer through this travel-headache that wouldn't ease, talking into a desk-mike about my mum and dad and cute baby sisters. Then my mum had come on and talked simultaneously of equations and integral calculus and the excitement of the music business until another radio show was over and we were on our way.

I was proud of my mum as she came on the radio talking like a maths teacher, a mother and a proper English lady. We were a curiosity, a mother with a pop star daughter, apparently a singing success in little England, where things, I felt, were very different. The radio stations knew nothing about

me, or my music. Mostly they played *Proud*, without expecting to play it again. Things were very different here. Here, I
was starting again, starting over, as the Americans would say.
I don't think they could see what there was to me. They did-
n't seem to get it.

'The next guest,' The Horse Whisperer whispered, hoarsely,
'on ol' Horse's Laid-Back Landslide Show, is here all the way
from London, England. She's called Amy Pepperpot –'
   'Peppercorn.'
   'Amy Peppercorn,' ol' Horse rasped, holding up one
mighty meaty finger, 'pardon me, young lady. So, how're
things across the pond there? London still swinging, is it?'
   'Swinging?' I managed to say.
   'Great!' he growled. 'Just great. Listen, you know who I
had, right here on this show, right there on that chair, over
from your country, only a very little while ago? You know?
Sid,' he said.
   'Sid?' I said.
   So far, I'd said three words: Peppercorn, swinging and Sid.
That was all I'd managed to say during this interview to the
great listening public of the city of Philadelphia.
   'Sid,' he said. 'Sid Vicious. Sid?'
   'Oh,' I said, still practising my monosyllabic non-answers.
   'Poor Sid,' he said.
   I said, 'Yeah,' thinking that we were about to bat one or
two words back and forth for the whole fifteen-minute inter-
view.
   'So, things are going well for you, over there in the UK?'
   I looked through the glass panel at my mum. 'Yes,' I said,
hoping Horse was going to ask my mum into the studio. She

might at least have something to say about poor vicious Sid. 'Yes. Everybody seems to be quite happy with the way things are going.'

'Oh?' he said.

I glanced at my mum again.

Horse blinked, slow and mule-like. 'Well, young lady,' he drawled, 'you certainly seem to've been having yourself a high old time. These here newspapers,' he said, producing a heap of Barry Bone's newsrags from a recess beneath his desk, 'they're full o' stuff, ain't they? It seems,' Horse seemed to turn and say to his microphone, 'that little Amy here's been whoopin' up a rare old time over there in England, ain't that right, little Amy?'

The pile of papers he'd produced thumped down between us, over a week's worth of *Daily Reader*s, with the latest headline on top:

AMY THREW PHONE FROM MOVING CAR WINDOW!

My mum's distressed face appeared clasped between her headphones like a pale moon captured in a pair of tongs. The colour was draining from her cheeks.

Mine were doing the opposite, I could feel, from the prickle and burn of anger mixed with embarrassment.

'Throwing phones out of cars,' Horse said, picking up and separating the pile on the table. 'Trashing hotel rooms.'

'Well, no,' I tried to say, 'that's just –'

'No? Parties – pretty wild, by the sound of them. Drugs –'

'No! That's not true!'

My mum's wan face was floating away from me. I glanced at her again, but she was too far away to help me.

'Hey, hey,' Horse was softly neighing. 'It's rock-and-roll little Amy. Come on; we ain't here to judge you.'

'No?' I glowed. I felt dizzy, with a jaw ache where I was clenching too tight.

'Hell, no. Party as hard as you can, that's our philosophy. You're in rock-and-roll, be rock-and-roll. Good on you, young lady. Let's keep the memory of Sid and Jimi and Kurt, why not?'

'Because – they're just –' I said, stumbling because I didn't know any of the people he was talking about. 'They're not me, are they?'

Ol' Horse laughed. 'No, they're sure not. But as long as you're out there doing the wild thing, that's what matters.'

'Does it?' I said.

'Yep,' Horse's teeth champed. 'Sure does.'

'New York still buzzing, is it?'

'We're in Philadelphia now,' I said.

'You pop stars!' Beccs said.

I didn't laugh, for once. I couldn't have felt less like a star. 'My mum's been doing almost as much of the interviews as I have,' I said.

'Lucky she's with you, then,' said Beccs.

'Yes, I'm lucky.'

'The papers are still on at you, though.'

'I know. We've seen them.'

'Out there?'

'Yeah. They come up all over the place. Hotels, radio stations. You don't have to bother telling me what they're saying.'

They appeared in the hotels, they came up on radio interviews; wherever we went, chasing radio stations manned by DJs Wolfe and Horse and other assorted large mammals.

Here was yet another read-all-about-it headline from home's past press, the super-soar-away *Daily Reader*:

AMY THREW PHONE FROM MOVING CAR WINDOW!

My mum followed Amy's exclamation-marked actions, without questioning me any further about what had happened between Jag and me. Yes, I had thrown his mobile phone, or rather dropped it into the road from the car when I found he'd been betraying me, helping Ray Ray control me, my emotions, my passions, my very thought processes. I had opened that car window and dropped the offending, offensive object with its Ray-gun stuttering messages into the road under the double wheels of the lorry trucking on behind; I had done this, but it was only fair, considering how I had been treated. Blaring out across a hotel lobby like that though, my actions appeared merely emotional, hysterically unreasonable, which was just *not* fair. They screamed at me in an English accent louder and more shrill than I could ever have shrieked, but wildly out of tune, in some kind of cacophony of strangled birds.

That was how it sounded to me, anyway. Wherever we went I could see the news headlines, I could hear the four and twenty blackbirds baked into a nightmare pie.

I had to call Beccs again:

'Have you spoken to Ben?'

'Yes.'

'Did he tell you if anyone's heard from Leo?'

'I don't know. I don't think so. Nothing since the papers. "She's so sweet, she's lovely." You'd think, if he liked you so much . . .'

My breathing was quickening, the turbine thudding in my ears growing louder. It was difficult to hear anything above the engines that never stopped, since the first plane had powered up – no, before that. Since Ben had burst my bubble of happiness that night we were alone in the Solar studio – no, even before that.

I woke up again. How many times? I didn't know. Sleeping was becoming so like waking, or not sleeping: same sound, same feelings.

'What?' I always found myself saying, waking, not sleeping. The hotel room surrounded me, pinning me back on the bed, drawing a gun, warning me not to move. Shadows shifted, lurching out of position. My heart was thumping.

My mum was in the room next to mine. I felt a bit like I was a little girl again. I wanted to knock on her door, go in with sleep in my eyes and climb into bed with her. She used to hold me after a nightmare. She held me whenever the amok beating of my heart had threatened and then turned into an epileptic fit. If I got to my mum early enough, sometimes she could hold off a seizure. Sometimes she could calm the electric-flicker of my eyes, letting out the heat from the mega-hertz madness flashing through my head. My mum could do this for me.

Oh, she's lovely, she's sweet but . . .

But. Dot, dot, dot. They could write whatever they liked about me. How could I ever get the chance to explain my flight from Jagdish, from the hotel in Cornwall? How was I supposed to let it be known how the tussle, the little shove, not fight, had happened between Ben and Adam?

In the night, thinking about it all, I seemed so nasty, so mean and selfish, that perhaps the papers were at least partly right?

I sweated in the night in an American dream hotel, sliding downhill, thinking of my crashing reputation thousands of miles away in the UK. I didn't deserve this, did I? Or did I?

Leo, I felt sure, wouldn't have wanted to hurt me like this. Poor Leo. Something like this – what it would do to him. Lovely Leo. He wouldn't have done this to me on purpose, surely, would he? Or would he?

*** Twenty

We were travelling back to New York for the last night of the tour, for the one television appearance that was that evening.

'Are you sure you're okay?' my mum was saying to me. 'Have you taken your medication?'

I thought of Jag every time she said that.

Mum insisted that the press furore, the madness in the papers couldn't last much longer. She pointed out how they had stopped calling me 'Little'. Amy Peppercorn they reported on now, so suddenly grown up and acting like a – like some kind of pop diva, thinking that everyone around her was put there to serve or amuse her. That was how they made me sound, as if I'd grown up overnight into a monster.

'Am I a monster?' I said to my mum.

The aeroplane back to New York roared round us. 'No,' she said, reaching forward, turning in her seat to hold me, 'no, of course you're not. Don't let them make you think badly of yourself.'

'It's so hard not to,' I said.

'Don't let them get to you. People don't think that of you.'

'Don't they?'

'No, they don't. You'll see. We'll be home in a couple of days. You'll see what it's really like, then.'

'I need to see Leo. He should have been here.'

'Yes, I know.'

'But you don't know what all this will do to him.'

'Don't I?'

'This is his life. Solar. Ray Ray.'

'Don't worry so much. Ray won't let anything happen to him.'

'Won't he?'

'No. There'll always be a place for Leo.'

'Will there, Mum? Are you sure?'

'Yes. Somewhere. I'm sure.'

I looked out of the window at New York. We were descending, but it seemed as if the great city were reaching up towards us with glittery silver arms, ready to drag us into itself until we were consumed by an apple too big to swallow. If there would always be a place for Leo, I really couldn't imagine where, now, it would be.

We had our car to take us straight to the studios. New York shines like a greedy parody of paradise on one block, until you turn the corner and trip over the trap where Paradise NY ends and the sick sidewalks begin. The yellow cabs kind of lurch, thumping down from one level as you pass from one vicinity to the other, provided the cab will even go there, bumping up again on your return.

Our car halted in a yellow sea of lurching, bumping cabs. One of the great bridges that spanned the Hudson River was blocked with cars and yellow cabs, with wildly gesticulating cab drivers blaming every other vehicle but their own. Everybody was in everybody else's way.

'I'll find a ways round,' our driver turned and said. We were back to being driven about by big Frank. 'There's always a ways round,' he said, before we made the bridge, turning out onto another massively wide road through another road-swept neighbourhood.

He turned the car again. Another road was blocked. He turned again. The New York brownstone buildings swept sideways across the front of the turning car. The hysterical wail of a police or ambulance siren was never far away. Blue lights flashed. There was some trouble up ahead. Somebody was hurt.

I didn't know where we were. My mum said she wanted to see where the twin towers of the World Trade Centre used to be. But they weren't anywhere. Nor were we. Everywhere I looked, they were not. I could only see here in negative terms, with our car smelling sickly of expensive upholstery and carpets, with the sirens blaring and lights flashing.

'We'll be there on time,' my mum said worriedly, looking at her watch. 'There's plenty of time yet.'

'Plenny-a time,' the driver echoed. 'Hey, this is New York. Shit happens, yeah? . . . Pardon me.'

Yeah, I was thinking, it happens in England, too. In London, it happens.

'Don't worry,' my mum said.

But I couldn't help but feel the engines thrumming all round me, aeroplanes, cars, cabs, ambulances. I felt it all happening, here, in London, where more papers were always being printed. My jaw had begun to ache. My teeth felt strange, as if they were about to come loose.

Then my mouth began to crumble, as if my teeth really were collapsing, falling to damp grey dust on the crust of my tongue. I bounced awake, realising only then that I had almost dropped off to city sleep in the city that didn't. The hooters, the American horns of impatience blared all round us as I checked my mouth for breakages, relieved to find my teeth in two neat upper and lower rows.

There was a tune playing in my head, some kind of dreadful nursery rhyme, telling of some horrific nursery crime, like a drunken fairground roundabout tune full of dark malevolence. I bounced back into a reality of cacophonous car-horns just as malevolent as the daytime nightmare I had just visited in unrestful sleep. I reached out to touch my mum just to be sure she was there, only to find that she wasn't there. I shot up on the big empty car seat.

'What's the matter?' my mum said, from my side, where she was, and had been all along.

'I –' I said. 'I –'

'Amy, are you all –'

'I fell asleep,' I said.

'We'll find a ways round,' the driver was still saying, repeating his mantra of hope. 'There's always a ways round.'

'Try to rest,' my mum said. 'Try to rest. Don't worry so much. It's all okay. Don't think about the papers.'

Above us, through the tinted glass solar-panelled roof, the sleepers of a girdered overhead railway flickered by, as if we were hanging by the body of our car, running along the underside of it.

'What do they know?' my mum was saying.

'Always a ways round,' repeated the driver.

'What do the papers know, anyway?' my mum said, from far away, in a voice that was almost, but not quite, hers. 'Amy threw the phone out of the window of the moving car,' her disappearing voice chanted. 'What do they know? *How* do they know?'

How *did* they know?

Something sharp touched me in the brain. Our car carried on, but in a different direction. The traffic and my dream stood in its way. We couldn't find a ways round them.

How did they know?

The sharp touch alerted me, bouncing me almost out of my car seat. We were all awake suddenly, clumping down or up one of those city class ramps, those money barriers wealth attempted to erect against crime and poverty in this separated, segregated city.

'What did you say?' I said to my mum.

She looked at me and smiled. 'I didn't say anything. You were asleep again, mumbling away'

'What did I say?' I said.

'I don't know,' she said, 'I couldn't quite hear.'

I couldn't, either. All I knew of what I'd said was that it must have made me feel quite sick. I swallowed, checking the rows of my teeth again, inspecting myself inside and out for whatever it was that was making me feel worse than ever.

My mum had been telling me not to worry about what the papers were saying back home. They were telling tales of how little spoilt grown-up Amy had thrown a phone from the window of a moving car.

That was It! How did they know about it? I hadn't told anybody about trashing Jag's phone, so he must have told them. But I hadn't told him I'd dropped it from the car. I hadn't told Jag those kinds of details, or my mum, or Leo, Ben, no one. No one, except . . .

Oh, how it happened, that sole-of-the-shoe stuff, here, at home, everywhere. Nowhere was safe: I had felt like that before, when I had discovered Ray Ray's web of control folding in and darkly cocooning me. But this, this stuff that happened, happened at the heart of me; threatening my heart's safety, threatening to break my heart's safety anchor to the past. I hadn't told anybody about dropping the phone from the window of the car. I hadn't told anybody. Nobody knew. Except me. Except me and . . .

'Mum,' I said, 'I don't feel very well.' After days of feeling it, I had finally to admit to feeling ill.

Nobody knew. Except me. Except me . . . and . . .

'Hey,' our driver said, 'we take the subway, yeah? We dump the car, we take the subway.'

'Yes,' my mum said, looking at me. 'We'll take the tube. You'll feel better.'

Nobody knew. It was a secret. I'd shared that secret, but nobody else was supposed to know!

'The toob?' our driver said.

Twenty-One

'**H**ey,' he said, 'I ged it. The toob! This is a toob, right? Hey, the toob!'

We sat in the subway station waiting for a train. I think our driver Frank was armed. His big black jacket bulged under one arm as if from a gun. He was large and relaxed, but watched everyone, closely, constantly.

I wanted to fall asleep. This city wanted to sleep, I was sure, it needed to, but never quite managed it. The city was always too aware of its own rumblings to doze off, too bristlingly itchy to lie back and just relax. As much as New York had a pounding headache, as much as the city's mouth tasted of bad pastrami and the dark dehydration of black coffee, still it would not, would not give in.

A toob-train arrived along the opposite platform, covered, every last millimetre, in graffiti. First of all, when the train arrives, it looks as if it's been purposely painted in every colour there is. Then the chaos of layer upon layer of graffiti signatures hits the eye like a headache.

My head did ache, frantically. The flicker-by of that overhead railway we'd driven along underneath still stuttered over the roll of my eyes. No more trains arrived at our underground station, although I could hear them clattering overhead. The railways were in the sky, they were underground. They were over us, they were under us.

We weakened, train-awaiting, head-holding commuters

were sandwiched over and under the epileptic repetition of sleepers and tracks, sleepers and tracks, sleepers and tracks, clackety-clack, clackety-clack. There was no thinking through it, no working it out. People didn't belong there, within the belly of the whale, incarcerated in a railway-cell of sleeper ribs, caged and confused by questions and no answers. I stood up.

'Amy,' my mum said, a world of concern in her voice.

I looked up the line into the darkness of the whale's belly. 'Will I have time to make a call?' I said.

Our driver unwrapped a stick of gum.

My mum looked at her watch.

'I need to speak to Beccs,' I said.

My mum peered into the face of her watch, trying to work out what time it was at home.

The driver shrugged. He always shrugged. His shoulders were piled so high, every movement seemed like a shrug.

I needed to speak to Beccs. We had shared secrets. She was where I put things, special things, secret things, the precious things between us, for safe-keeping. I needed them kept safe. I needed Beccs.

But the grinding graffiti of our train crashed metal on metal behind my back as my mum looked up and said something, something terrible. Something like, through the grind of train noise, 'You can't rely on her being there.'

Or, 'She won't always be there for you.'

Or, 'She's not there for that.'

Or, 'She's not for you, or keeping your secrets.'

Something like that.

Or some other refusal against the side of the train with the hissing doors opening and the striped snake of carriages waiting to receive us and take us down and down.

Our car driver's black jacket flapped as he stooped to stand up from his seat. For the confusion of a moment, I saw the slick black of his belt and shoulder holster. Metal on gun-metal.

When we left the subway, the toob, we still had quite a walk to the TV studio. My mum was hoping it would clear my head.

We stopped for a Coke. The coldness of the mass of ice over which it came poured hit me just above one eye with an extra, extra-unwelcome pain. Outside the deli we'd stopped at, a huge newsstand shouted out across the sidewalk. I wanted to look for a London paper; my mum found one for me, folded it and quickly paid too much for it.

'Let's go,' she said. 'It's late.'

Frank, our driver, now our minder, our bodyguard, looked at his watch. He squared his shoulders, like an armed boxer shifting inside his shoulder-holster straps.

'Let me see the paper,' I said.

'Let's go,' my mum said again. 'It's very late.'

The bodyguard chewed over another look at his wrist-watch. 'Hey, y'know, guys, it's kinda –'

'Let me see the paper,' I said.

My mum hurried up the pavement, the sidewalk. New Yorkers bustled on by in both directions with a particular concentration on the pavement-sidewalk that seemed unbreakable. There was business to be done here, and these were the people to be doing it.

Standing still against the flow of passers-by, with my minder armed with a hidden handgun beside me, I had the feeling of motion, like when you look at the sea washing round your ankles and you seem to be moving down the beach rather than the tide up: I stood against the tide, demanding to see the London newspaper that my mother was so determined to keep away from me. 'Mum!' I called.

She stopped. The tide washed round her. She turned to look back at me.

'Mum. Please let me see it.'

Nobody seemed to notice us, stationary, as we were, on the hurrying sidewalk. We could not have been in London. I didn't know where else we might have been standing, where else looked and felt and smelt like this, but not London. Not England or anywhere else I'd visited in the UK. Which was almost everywhere. On tour, I had seen just about everywhere there, but not this.

'Please let me see the paper,' I said.

My mum walked towards me. 'You'd be better off – after the show.'

But she didn't stop me from taking the paper from under her arm. I opened it. All my secrets were out, doing damage.

The driver beside me had a gun. He didn't have to fire it. But somebody was damaged, anyway. Somebody, not just me, for once, was in imminent danger.

***⋆ Twenty-Two

Although I was a stranger, I was a welcome visitor here, here to do a song, put in an appearance, to perform for American audiences in the studio and on TV. But I didn't feel new to this place, at all. I felt as if I'd been here before. The accent had changed, but the TV studio protocol was the same.

The newspaper headlines had hit me above the eye even more effectively than the cold, iced Coke. It wasn't what I'd been expecting, anticipating, as I was, more of my intimacies spread, splayed, displayed cover to cover for inspection and gratification. I'd been cringingly anticipating my Beccs-kept secrets revealed in appallingly large script for front and inner page titillation. Instead, instead, I cringed. What next? What could even my mum have done to have prevented any of this?

My mum, protected by a gun, trying to protect me, had hustled us along the bustling street and into the over-warm welcome of the local TV station. Everybody knew me there. They were familiar with my songs, my records, my success. Everybody told me how much they liked me.

We were late. Not too late, just late. I had to go straight into make-up. This was TV. Make-up comes at you, thick and hard. My eyebrows became accentuated and tilted, more arched, making me appear more amused than the newspaper report would have ever allowed.

'What you singin', honey?'

'Love Makes Me Sick.'

They laughed. Whenever I said the title of that song, laughter bit the uptown air.

My mum had disappeared in the warm hurry to have me made up, dressed and made ready for my performance. She wrested the offence of yesterday's news from my grip before she went. Then she was gone with the paper, but leaving the news still fisted in my palms and gripping fingers.

I needed to speak to someone. I needed to speak. I needed to.

I needed.

Needed.

A mouth was painted on over my own, my eyes exaggerated but disguised.

The newspaper had disappeared with my mum, both taken from me. My mum would always be there for me; but so would the news. Not once had I managed to separate this city from the bad-news capital headlines publicising intimacies told in confidence, or the damage resulting from them. I'd shared my secrets with – with just one person. And now – now the engines of destruction pounded against the front of my brain. One thing always led to another; in that way, only I could be held responsible for that terrible, dreadful newspaper headline.

*** Twenty-Three

AMY PEPPERCORN MINDER IN DRUGS COMA DRAMA!
Your Super-Soaring-Sonic Daily Reader Exclusive
By Barry Bone

Singing sensation Amy Peppercorn's personal assistant and music arranger, Mr Leo Sanderson, was discovered yesterday in a drugs-induced coma in a hotel room in the southwest of England. He was rushed to a local hospital, but was later transferred by helicopter to an intensive care unit in a specialist London clinic.

Ms Peppercorn, on tour in America, has not been available for comment.

Twenty-Four

The show was going out live. It was on early, so perhaps there wouldn't be too many people watching. I didn't mind, because this performance wasn't likely to be anything like one of my best. Worst, most likely.

I felt my teeth, as if they had surface nerves, like my face, with that huge ache above the eye without any ice cream or cold Coke to blame.

'I think you're ready,' my make-up artist was saying, looking at my face in the mirror. From where she saw me, she missed my frightened teeth, the synthetic slant of my eyebrows. She couldn't see me, not from there, not mirrored for TV as I was, happily painted, painted happy.

It had all gone wrong again. The news was collapsing from bad to worse. My mum had told me I shouldn't see the headlines from Britain, but I could: all the way from Britain. They contained too much simple truth, for once. For once and for all.

'Yes,' the make-up artist said, 'very nice. I think you're needed in wardrobe.'

In wardrobe, a very strange, but perfectly fitting outfit was waiting for me. I stepped into this kind of Lincoln green, almost Robin Hood type skirt and top with little green boots and a very bizarre hat like an air hostess, also distinctly green. I looked like an elf, a pixie.

'Hey,' they were saying, the girls in wardrobe with me,

'you look adorable. Simply adorable! Doesn't she, Vern?'

'Simply adorable!' Vern exclaimed. They had the most incredibly elaborate hand-movements, as if they were constantly in some kind of animated argument on prime-time TV, sensationally soapy and melodramatic.

'That colour! Oh my God!'

'How'd you feel, honey?'

'Oh, she feels good, don't you, babe? How could you feel anything but good, when you look like that?'

'And you're a singer, aren't you?'

'Oh, my God, is she?'

'Yeah. In England.'

'Oh my God! Do you know Courtney Schaeffer, honey?'

'Yes, I do, actually.'

'Oh my God – that accent!'

'You know Courtney? I know Courtney! Isn't she great? She was here, in – what – May? Isn't she just great!'

'Oh my God!'

'Yeah!'

Yeah, yeah, yeah. But I didn't mind. Or rather I didn't care, about anything. I did, but not about what was being said. I cared about what had been written, how and when it had happened to him. And why.

I'd been there before, standing on a little stage, maybe not dressed so impishly, but I'd felt like this, waiting for my turn, for the lights to come on, music to start. I'd have to start singing, as soon as all that happened. Which meant finding a breath, a decent gulp of air from somewhere. The elfin uniform was too tight around my ribcage. The spotlights were too harsh, too hot. I was far too hot. There were dark little dots and squirms cavorting from the corners of my eyes, or some dreadful newsprint reproduced there, just out of reading distance.

Something was wrong, had gone wrong. Back in the UK, here, something dreadfully wrong. The wrong people were taking the blame. I felt – I think – sick: almost sick, at that breathless point before actually throwing up.

But the lights were coming on. Now was not the time to puke, or even think. Now was the time to breathe, as the lights blinked and the studio audience applauded. I heard them as if from somebody's TV in the next room. The lights were digging me in the eyes. My eyes were throbbing with the cold heat of ice cream I hadn't eaten, my nose fizzing with burped cola. My pre-taped music was playing, as if to trigger me. I looked up.

Something shifted.

I had to sing. *Love Makes Me Sick*:

Falling down all over the place
Shaking like a lunatic
A look of madness on my face
Something's making me feel sick.

Walking round in a haze
Talking too loud and much too quick,
Through restless nights and dog-tired days
You're making me feel – making me –
Feel . . .

. . . feel – like an – as if – as the music disintegrated into the throb of sound fuzz, as my head went full ice-flow and my eyes flew up into the ice head and I think – I thought I was about to have a seizure. It felt like it; all the old symptoms were there in the electrical pulse of my face and eyes.

146

You're making me feel – making me –
Feel . . .

. . . as if, as if a seizure was coming, as if I was about to hit the ground running, grinding, grounded, gnashing and thrashing. All the little devils of seizure flew before my eyes in a swirling storm as my breath quickened with the pounding of my pulse.

You're making me feel . . .

I felt as if – however I felt, I faltered, halting, falling silent as the song continued without words. 'Wait a minute,' I said, although I couldn't be sure if anybody heard me.

If I were about to have an epileptic seizure, it would have to be a strange one. Although my heart was racing, my electric eyes flickering, I myself stood, still able to think, to feel, to start to fight back.

The music ground to a halt, but I didn't. No, I didn't. There were too many newspaper reports against me, too many secrets spoiled, too many friends in jeopardy. The latest headlines were all about Leo, but about me too. Love was making me feel sick, so I started to feel angry. I shook my head, gritting my teeth. The cameras were pointed at me, their LED indicators blinking. The studio audience awaited my next move.

I threw off the little green cap they'd given me, gripping the microphone in its stand, unclipping it. 'Go again!' I cried.

Nothing happened.

So I started to sing:

But I'd rather feel
So very ill

Than never be in love at all.
Yes, I'd rather feel
So very ill
Than never be in love at all.

But this time in anger, kicking back, defending, attacking. No seizure, no epileptic failure. Something had to happen. I was about to make it happen.

Love makes me sick
But I can't take a pill
Love makes me sick
I must like being ill
Love makes me sick
And it gives me such a thrill.

I'd rather feel so very ill: I didn't care. Nobody, but nobody was going to do this to me, to the people I cared most about.

Yes, I'd rather feel so very ill than never be in love at all. I had too much love in me to be beaten this easily. Too much, far too much love to let things happen, to let Barry Bone beat me, to let so much suffering go by unchallenged.

But I'd rather feel
So very ill
Than never be in love at all.
Yes, I'd rather feel
So very ill
Than never be in love at all.

Love makes me sick
But I can't take a pill
Love makes me sick

I must like being ill
Love makes me sick
And it gives me such a thrill.

My voice had taken on new elements: rage, outrage, strength. All of these things perhaps. Perhaps just sheer anger.

The audience didn't know what had hit them. I just flew at them, striking them round the face with my voice, the sincerity of my passion.

And it gives me such a thrill.

As the song ended, as I clipped the hand mike back into its stand, I looked up at a studio of shocked faces. They didn't know whether to cry or clap.

They clapped, tumultuously. They didn't cry. Neither did I. I clenched my fists, raising my hands into the air in victory. I was the winner. Nobody, but nobody was going to beat me now!

✯✯✯ Twenty-Five

My mum thought I shouldn't have been flying, not straight away, but I was afraid I'd be too late. 'You're so tired,' she said. 'Just take a couple of days out. Why won't you? We could have some fun in New York again.'

I wanted to do as my mum suggested. It would have been good, so good to enjoy the extra time out with her. And yes, I was tired. But more than all this, more than anything, I had to get back, go home. Find out.

'I really think,' she said, looking at me worriedly, 'you should have a look at what happened to you, on the video.'

'Why,' I said, trying to make a joke of it, 'didn't they have it on DVD?'

'You know what I mean. I'll play you the recording. You can see for yourself. I should never have allowed you to – '

'You didn't allow me anything, Mum. I did it. You weren't to know how I was feeling.'

'But I should have,' she said. 'I should have seen it coming.'

'Seen what coming? I'm fine. It's time to leave, that's all.'

'I really thought you were about to have a seizure,' she said.

'Well,' I said, 'I wasn't. I'm fit. The medication works. I wasn't having a seizure.' It was sickness, simply; plane sickness, travel, car and toob sickness, New York sore sickness, plain and simple. But more than this, I was having a crisis of confidence. Now I had the confidence to overcome the crisis.

I suppose should have been resting, like my mum said. But Lovely Leo was in intensive care in a clinic in London and I had to get back there. I told my mum I'd rest on the plane.

She didn't like it, not one bit.

No rest. Plenty of orange juice, my medication, of course, but no rest; with the wing jet engines roaring in my inner ears, trying to relax in another plane seat with too many people glancing back at me with a different kind of look of recognition. At least, that's how it seemed to me, as I was popping with jagged nerve-ends, trying to avoid another aeroplane headache.

The jet engines still whistled non-stop from JFK to Heathrow, the bustling crowds in baggage reclaim looking up from the empty conveyer belts at me, then straight back down again.

On the American side of the Atlantic, the post 9/11 security procedures kept us queuing for hours, buzzing with frustration, tired and testy but determined to get through. On the UK side, baggage reclaim informed us with blank screens that we were going nowhere in a hurry. But I was in a desperate rush, funnelling through a tube of urgency to get back to all the landslide situations I now felt I should never have left.

Something about the electric power short-circuit of my near-seizure had focused my mind. Although I did feel physically depleted, my mind drove forward, looking for resolutions, determined to understand where I stood. The press and the public were one thing to worry about, but more importantly, there was Leo, lying unconscious in a clinic as a direct result of. . . . whatever.

And then – the other thing.

My best f –

'Amy,' my mum said, for the umpteenth time, watching me warily, worrying over my health and state of mind. She knew about Leo. She knew nothing about the secrets that had been given away, perhaps sold, who knows, to the money-fluttering gutter press.

Who had done this to me?

Who was in a position to hold such sellable secrets, and then not hold them?

'I have to go,' I said. 'I can't wait any longer.'

The screens were still conspicuously blank, the baggage conveyers still and silent.

'What?' my mum said. 'You're not going anywhere with-out – '

But I was on my way, walking away from my mum's concerns towards concerns of my own. She started to follow me. 'No,' I said, stopping us both. 'Stay there, Mum. You get the luggage. I'll get a cab. Leo's in a – it's time to go!'

'Amy, no!'

'Mum, yes!'

My mum and I had never spoken to each other like that before. After the TV show in New York, all I'd managed to say was, 'I want to go home.'

My mum's face had been waiting for me to calm down after my passionate stage performance. She'd smiled at me. 'We will,' she'd said.

But I had said again, 'I want to go home.'

From that moment of emergence, I had been insistent, unyielding, demanding. My mum had humoured me: 'Yes, darling, we'll go home.'

She had smiled still, underestimating my resolve. Soon I had turned her smile of understanding to confused worry. No, I would not take my time to rest. No, I would not see a doctor. No, I wasn't waiting any longer, even a day. Not another hour, or minute, if I could possibly help it. If my mum wouldn't call the airport for the next flight, then I would.

All the way through honking yellow cab races to security-locked Kennedy, to the turbulent tarmac under our at-long-last lifting aeroplane, through turbine whine and jet-fuel stench and head-set blare of unsatisfactory, factory music and faulty films we had kept the peace. But now, we stood looking at each other, ignoring all the other plane passengers watching us as they waited for their bags to appear.

'Amy, no!'

'Mum, yes!'

My mum had never been one to shout at her children. She was far more intelligent than that. From where I stood staring, with the blind-spot devils of darkness still leaping at the corners of my eyes, I could determine my mother's calculations, her daughter-directed mathematics of care and confidence. In the end I saw her innate intelligence give way across an equals sign, from care to confidence. She didn't give up on me; she'd never do that. She merely allowed me, with a single, ever so slight shift of expression, to turn and walk away.

I walked away. I loved my mum more than ever, I think, but I had to get away from her and see to the things she could no longer help me with.

✶✶✶ Twenty-Six

The clinic receptionist looked back down, then up again. 'He's down the hall, in room twenty. I'll just check to see who the duty nurse is.' She picked up a telephone. 'Yes,' she said, looking at me, 'Miss Peppercorn's right here. She wishes to visit . . . I don't know. Perhaps you'd better ask her?' She hung up. 'Sister will be right with you. If you'd care to wait over there, she'd like to ask you something.'

Over there, straight from the airport to the clinic in a cab, smelling of transatlantic travel, I waited and wondered what the Sister could possibly want to ask me about Leo. As I waited, I checked my mobile for messages.

'Miss Peppercorn,' the Sister said.

I leapt.

The Sister had appeared suddenly, a surprisingly young woman in a starched white hospital-drama uniform.

'Is he – is he conscious?' I stumbled, quickly tucking away my blank mobile phone.

'Oh – yes, of course. He's been having lunch.'

I breathed, sighed. 'Oh, lunch? Is he – how is he? I thought – '

'A coma?' she smiled. 'The press. You know what they're like. He was unconscious when they found him. He did need just a little bit of close care.'

'But he's all right?'

'Well, physically, yes. He's upset, of course.'

She led me along the corridor. 'What did he have for lunch?' I asked.

She smiled. 'I'm not sure. Pasta, I think. Does it matter?'

'It matters to Leo,' I said.

'Pasta's good. It'll build his strength up.'

I smiled now. 'I don't think Leo would see it that way. Anyway, what was it you wanted to ask me? The receptionist said you wanted –'

'Oh, yes. I wanted to ask you – would it be possible – would you mind if I could just have your autograph? For my little boy?'

Lovely Leo was crying. He was sitting up in bed, lunch barely touched on a discarded tray on the chair, while I sat on the bed beside him, holding him. He cried softly. If I hadn't finished with crying, if all my tears hadn't run dry, I'd have wept with him.

'I'm sorry, Lovely,' he sobbed. 'I'm so sorry.'

'No, Leo. No need to be sorry.'

He cried some more, before prising free of my head-hold to fumble for a box of paper tissues from the bedside cabinet. 'I'm getting through a box of these an hour,' he said. 'I can't stop.'

'That's all right,' I said. 'It's a good thing, sometimes, to cry. You're a man –'

'Am I?' he looked up, almost shocked. 'Oh my, so I am.'

For a moment I saw the old, the lovely, self-mocking Leo come to the surface. 'My dad could never cry,' I said. 'I can't imagine it, anyway.'

He blew his nose, extremely loudly. 'Oh, dear. You'll have to take no notice. I cried over *Corrie* last night, and I'm not even joking. There's no end to it, once I start. I've got every man's tears, I have.'

'You've got my dad's,' I said.

'I've got every man's. What about Ray's? Can you imagine that?'

I tried. Ray crying: Raymond Raymond having a proper sob. 'No,' I said, 'I can't imagine that at all.'

'Well,' he said, looking at me strangely, 'you'd be wrong. You don't know him,' he started, breaking down again, reaching for more tissues.

'Leo,' I said.

'I'm so sorry,' he sobbed. 'How can I –'

'Leo, you don't have to –'

'I do. Yes, I do. I couldn't do anything to stop it happening. Before I knew anything, there it all was, all over the papers.'

'It doesn't matter.'

'Yes, it does. Lovely, it matters. Everything matters.'

'Leo, listen to me. Did you talk to Barry Bone?'

Leo dabbed his cheek with a tissue. 'Lovely,' he said, 'of course I did.'

'You did?'

'Of course. We have to talk to the press.'

'Yes, but –'

'No, Lovely, listen to me now. We cannot afford to just ignore people like Barry Bone. We have to give them something, if we're ever going to control what's being said or written. Do you understand?'

I nodded.

But Leo shook his head. 'No, you don't. I talked to him, you see, about nothing. I gave Barry Bone my usual spiel. You know me, I can go on and on forever without ever actually saying anything. That's what I do, Sweet.'

'Yes,' I said. 'I do understand.'

Leo wasn't crying. 'I told them how lovely you are,' he said.

We were looking at each other. Looking at each other. He wasn't going to say anything more. 'That's why it sounded so like you, in the reports,' I said.

'Oh, Lovely,' he sighed. 'Oh, Sweet.'

'I know, Leo, I know.'

'Do you, Lovely?'

I didn't know what to say next. 'Why didn't you tell me it wasn't you?'

He shrugged, without taking his eyes from mine. 'Why? Couldn't you see it?'

'Leo,' I said, reaching for his hand, 'I'm so sorry.'

'Don't,' he said. 'You'll set me off again.'

'Tell me what happened,' I said.

He looked at me quizzically.

'This,' I said, indicating the bed, and through it, everything that had happened to bring him to it.

'Oh,' he said, 'it's so stupid. A stupid mistake.'

'A mistake?'

'My pills. You know I can never sleep. I just forgot how many I'd taken.'

'You forgot?'

He shrugged. 'Maybe I didn't care to remember,' he said.

We stopped speaking for a while. The silence was too much to bear. 'Ray said you were out,' I said.

'Ray? Did he?'

'Was that it, Leo? Was that what – '

But Leo shook his head again. 'You don't know – you just don't know what Ray's like. He won't let me go. He'll never let me go. One way or the other, Ray doesn't do that. That's the trouble. If I could just – just . . .'

He halted.

'Leo, I –'

'No, Lovely, it doesn't matter –'

'But it does! It does!'

'Sweet, you can't change anything.'

'I let you down.'

'Because you were let down. I know, I know. Come here,' he said, holding out his arms, with his tears freely flowing. 'Come here, please.'

I held him. 'Leo,' I whispered, 'I'm here now. You didn't speak to the press, I know that for sure, but somebody did.'

'Yes,' he whispered.

'Yes,' I breathed. 'Yes,' but without saying what I thought I knew.

We held each other, a long, long time. We were trying to forgive. We were both trying not to feel let down.

Leo was lovely. He'd be going home in the morning. Home, for Leo: that made me realise that I didn't know where the place he called home was. I don't think I'd even remembered his surname was Sanderson, until I read it in the paper. Leo was just Leo. In fact, I wasn't sure if I'd ever known his full name. He was just – Lovely. And vulnerable: more vulnerable than I was, now. He'd told me once that I had to learn how not to give, because everything would surely be taken from me. I'd learned, but Leo was vulnerable, a lovely person giving and giving and receiving so very little in return.

'Everybody's letting everybody else down,' I said. 'We're all so – Leo, none of us can stand together against – against all the things we should be fighting. There's just too much.'

'No,' he said, 'that's not true. Somebody's done this to you. Who is it?'

I looked down at my mobile phone. It was no longer switched off, as it had been all the while in America.

'Who is it?' Leo was asking.

I looked at my phone.

'Amy?'

Leo said that. Amy? He caught me off guard, coming out with my name like that. From him, Amy was like a term of endearment, rare and lovely, special and very caring. I almost – I very nearly – I wanted not to cry; it was so hard, trying not to. So very hard. Lovely Leo calling me Amy like that very nearly defeated me, very nearly brought me to the almost-nothing of tears.

'Don't leave me, Leo,' I said. 'I've got to go now. Don't you leave me. Promise me. Promise me?'

'Sweet, I can't.'

'Leo,' I said. Nothing more. We looked at each other, wordlessly, for a long, long time.

✳✳✳ Twenty-Seven

On the Saturday streets of London, nobody noticed me in the back of a black cab, with my fame fading fast, becoming almost transparent against the empty intensity of the newspapers. Even the cabbie didn't seem to recognise me.

From the super-soar-away *Daily Reader*:
AMY THREW PHONE FROM MOVING CAR WINDOW!

AMY PEPPERCORN MINDER IN DRUGS COMA DRAMA!
Your Super-Soaring-Sonic Daily Reader Exclusive
By Barry Bone

Text to Beccs:
'DID YOU TALK TO BARRY BONE?'

'Of course I did,' Ben said.

The three girls, the Static Cats, were back for yet another try. Ben had rearranged some of their stuff and worked on their stage act with them. They were being given a second chance. And for the second time, they were pinning themselves nervously against the wall at the sight and sound of me. I must have looked a mess. And they must have thought there were always cat-fights going on in the studios, involving, in one way or another, Ben and me.

'Of course I talked to Barry Bone,' Ben said. 'Everybody talks to Barry Bone.'

'Why?'

'You can't get rid of the little – he's a slug, a worm. He worms his way in.'

'So you talk to him.'

'Yeah, I talk to him. You want to know what I tell him?'

I braced myself. Not for what Ben was likely to say to me, but because my mobile beeped, receiving a picture message. I breathed in sharply.

'I tell him where to go,' Ben said. 'That's what I tell Barry Bone. I tell him where to get off.'

I found myself holding my breath.

'Besides,' Ben said, 'what do I know? How could I tell Barry Bone anything? I don't know anything.'

'No,' I said, breathing uneasily, fishing out my phone. There it was: a picture message from Beccs in response to my text, waiting to be opened, waiting to show me what I suspected was true. 'You didn't know about any of that stuff in the papers, Ben, I know you didn't.'

Ben looked over and signalled with a wave to the Static Cats that he wouldn't be much longer.

'And neither did Leo,' I said.

'Didn't he?' Ben shrugged, perfectly uninterested.

'No,' I said, pressing the button on my mobile, 'he didn't.'

'Who did then?' Ben said.

I looked at the picture on my phone. It was the one I'd

sent to Beccs, the one I'd taken that afternoon outside our school.

'Who did?' Ben said.

'Do you know who this is?' I said, handing him the phone.

He looked at it, merely glancing at it. 'That's him,' he said, looking up. 'That's Barry Bone.' Then he looked again. 'And that's – James Benton, isn't it?'

He looked back at me. I nodded. He glanced at the picture once again. 'Ah,' he said.

'Yes,' I said. 'Ah.'

Raymond Raymond sat at his huge desk, writing. For a few moments, he didn't see me. He had his tongue out on one side of his mouth, like a little boy concentrating. Then some ghastly, demonic sixth sense informed him of my presence, as he looked up from his papers, his dark eyes like black beads under his lowered brow. 'Back, early.'

I stood in his doorway, looking an absolute mess.

He straightened. 'Okay, yeah?'

'Yeah,' I said. 'Okay.'

He stared at me, saying nothing.

'How's Leo?' I said.

He continued staring at me, as if he was never going to speak again.

'It's not what – ' I said, faltering, wanting to tell Ray what it was he didn't understand, while not wanting to tell Ray anything. 'It wasn't how it seemed – with Leo, and the papers.'

Ray took a breath. When Ray inhaled like that, he made it feel as if he were about to deprive you of oxygen, as if he was

162

trying to make you faint. 'Nothing's ever as it seems,' he said, breathing out. He stared at me some more. I tried to stare back. 'Good reports back,' he said, finally. 'From over there.'

'Good?'

'Great, in fact. Good telly. Pathos. Passion. Great stuff. The Yanks liked it. They liked your mum. And you.'

'That's more than they do here,' I said, 'at the moment.'

'The papers?' he said. And smiled! I could hardly believe it; Ray was smiling at me. There was hardly a time when Ray had bothered looking at me as if I was a person, not just his property. He smiled! 'I told you, you're in the news, girl. Either way, all's good. It doesn't matter. Your album's just gone to number one.'

The smile stayed, stuck to his face.

I tried to match him, stare for stare, smile for smile. 'I'll tell Leo,' I said.

'I told him,' Ray said.

I wondered again what Leo had meant when he said I didn't know Ray because I couldn't imagine Ray crying. Nobody could have imagined Ray crying, surely, could they?

'I want to go back,' I said. 'To the States.'

He nodded, his smile fading. Now we were talking business. 'Essential,' he said.

'But I'll not go back without Leo,' I said.

Ray stared – Ray stared.

'We can't go everywhere, just my mum and me,' I said. 'I need – I can't keep doing it like that.'

He sat back. 'No,' he said. 'You can't.'

Twenty-Eight

'It was me,' Beccs said.

She sounded empty, as if she had been crying. She wasn't crying now. Neither was I. I was being driven home from Solar through London, home again, with my mobile phone pressed to my ear.

'They found out everything, you're right,' Beccs said. 'How else could they have known? Of course it was me.'

'But you – ' I said, exasperated. 'You – ' I wanted to scream, but my voice was evaporating with me as we failed to appear to the busy contra-flow of pedestrians on the pavement. The tube ran thumping through under their feet somewhere underneath these English sidewalks, our own subway trains grinding metal on metal, one fearful noise, both sides of the Atlantic Ocean. My teeth ground like the Underground, here, there.

'I've let you down,' Beccs said.

'Beccs,' I said, 'I don't understand.'

My whole life, everything I most valued, the one real friend I had to cling to against the rolling insanity of what I did for a living, Beccs. She'd come to mean so much to me.

'I don't understand,' I said, although I thought I did, even as I was saying I didn't. Nothing could have lived up to my hopes and expectations indefinitely. Life wasn't like that. Whenever I was up, whenever it felt good to be me, something, *something* would always happen along to knock me back then try to kick me when I was down.

'I know,' Beccs said, although I suspected that she didn't. When I said I didn't understand, I thought I did, and when Beccs said she knew, I thought she didn't. That was what we'd come to between us, so suddenly. How? So suddenly – so very, horribly of a sudden. 'Amy,' she said, 'I don't know what to say – I don't know what to say to you, Amy.'

Then, of a very horrible sudden, she was gone. My mobile phone had lost her signal. So had I.

I felt like screaming. I didn't. I felt like crying. I didn't do that, either. Beccs – my whole life! All my secrets, given away by her! Everything between us, gone! Given, thrown away. Sold. Cheapened. Barry Bone had got to her through James Benton. But Beccs had let him in. Beccs had opened up and let the worm in.

'There you are!' my dad said, chirpily. He hugged me and kissed the top of my head. 'All sorted now?' he said.

All sorted? 'Yes,' I said. 'All done.'

'Your mum's got your things,' he said. 'She's not long back herself. Had to wait ages for the luggage. She's upstairs with the girls. Go and see her, then come back down and tell me all about America. – Hey, what about the album, eh?'

'Yeah,' I said, going out.

The twins ran at me, jostling each other to be the first to leap at me. 'Amy Peppercorn!' they cried. They were so funny when they did things like that, running about shouting my full name.

'Jo and Georgie Peppercorn!' I cried. But tried not to cry. Tried very, very hard not to.

My mum stood in her bedroom doorway watching me. 'How is he?' she said, meaning Leo. She knew – I was struggling, she knew. She knew how much I would have loved to go to her, after our trip together, after the understanding she'd shown me in the airport – go to her, run to her and let my mum see to it for me.

But she knew I wouldn't do it. This struggle, this particular struggle in me was going to have to be mine to deal with, on my own. Alone.

'Leo's going to be all right,' I said.

The girls ran off into my mum's room. She let them by without a glance, without breaking her eye-contact with me.

She didn't break it, I did. I turned away. My mum couldn't help me with this one. Beccs – Beccs, my whole life! Look at what she'd done, as I had to look at it, then look again, and again, until I couldn't see for looking, for the withheld tears filling, then falling. Tears falling.

Falling and falling.

✱✱✱ Twenty-Nine

The trip to America had made me see just how used to – how dependent I had become on Leo's lovely flapping fuss to flatter and fire me up before a show. He was showbiz to the bone, as he so often exclaimed, self-mockingly. How I needed Leo's ways, his silly little songs, his ditties, as he called them. I needed his fuss and nonsense, with such wonderful advice interwoven with rubbish so intensely that it was often only much later that the wisdom of what he'd said flopped into the open; and the wonder was just how I'd managed to overlook it in the first place.

'Sweet,' he'd said, sitting with me in his beautiful flat, sipping cups of mint tea, 'Lovely, you'll never even notice I'm not there.'

'That's not true. Leo, you've been there for me the whole time. I haven't been anywhere without you.'

'Only America.'

'No, not even there. You were with me, all the time. Or what I can remember of it. It was like a dream – like somebody else's dream.'

'Mine, actually, Lovely.'

'There you are, then. We're going back there, Leo, you and me.'

'No we're not, Sweet. It's time I was, you know, moving on, as they say.'

'Yes, and don't you always hate it when they say that?'

'Sweet, it's time. It's all becoming so, so very unhealthy. Not for you – you shine. For me. I'm shrivelling up. I have to get away.'

'It's nothing to do with Ben, is it.'

'No! Not at all. Ben? Good heavens! That boy?'

'It's Ray, then.'

'No, Lovely, it's me. I'm finished. Leo's out. It's time. I've cried it all away.'

'Oh, Leo!'

'No, Lovely, don't. Come here, come here. My goodness, but you're a star. You are! Don't let them stop you.'

'Leo, I need you with me.'

'Just give me a hug, Lovely.'

I shook my head. 'I thought you'd always be with me.'

'Not always, surely?'

I nodded. 'I thought you were – Leo. You know. Lovely Leo.'

I had thought Leo was – just Lovely.

And I had thought my best friend secure. I had felt secure in her, that we were watertight together, bomb-proof.

I'd thought Ben another danger threatening; but he caught me unawares with kindness in the corridor at Solar nearly a week after my return from America. 'I know what's happened,' he said. 'I know how that slime-Bone operates. I had a quiet word with him, and with James Benton – '

Ben looked kind and calm, but what he was saying worried me. 'Ben!' I said. 'You weren't – '

'Don't be silly,' he laughed. 'What do you take me for? James and I had a chat. He said he didn't realise he'd be causing you so many problems. Barry Bone offered him a lot of money.'

'And he took it.'

'Yeah, he took it. Beccs slapped his face, don't worry.'

'Beccs? Did she? Have you spoken to her?'

'No. I tried her mobile. Couldn't get through. Have you?'

'No.' I couldn't get through either. I hadn't actually tried to ring back after my mobile had lost her signal that day; I just couldn't do it. I couldn't do it. The chain of whispers linking my best, my worst and my most intimate experiences to the popular press were forged from the lips of my best friend, not broken by a simple slap round her boyfriend's face.

'No,' I said.

We were silent for a few moments. Usually, silence with Ben was filled with his anger, his pain and frustration. Now though, the silence spoke of my simple answer to his question, my one word halt in communications with Beccs. For almost a week we had not spoken or contacted each other in any way. Before, we hardly went a day without at least a text, a simple message to confirm over and over that we were still there for each other. Now the silence between Ben and I sounded exactly like a beautiful friendship dying, fading away without so much as a whimper.

'Call her,' Ben said, so quietly I very nearly failed to hear.

I heard. It killed me, not calling her; it did. 'How come you're suddenly in a position to start giving me advice?' I said.

Ben smiled. 'Just do it, Amy. Don't let Barry Bone in. Just wipe the slime away.'

I smiled. 'It's not just that,' I said.

'Amy,' he said, softly, 'I know what it is.' He shrugged. 'I've been, you know, seeing someone. You know – the man

169

who helped your dad? I go and talk, that's all. He helps me –
understand. I'm getting to be a real expert understander.'

He made me laugh. Ben, and he was making me laugh!

'No,' he said, smiling, 'I'm learning how to be honest.
With myself. I've still got a future, you know?'

'I know,' I said.

'Well then,' he said, as if he'd proved something.

Maybe he had. I just didn't know.

Next morning, an article in the *Daily Reader*:

OUR AMY FIGHTING FIT FOR US! by Barry Bone.
OUR AMY by Barry Bone!

Thirty

The Eiffel Tower: under it, in front of it, or behind it, whichever is the front and back, I don't think anybody knows, is a park. An open green space. That night, it was neither open nor green. It was covered, totally, in the milling, somehow orderly confusion that is many, many people. It seemed impossible that the crowd was French; they were every nation.

My mum came with me to Paris. So did my dad and my two little sisters. We wanted to make it a family outing. We were going to do the sights, including the Eiffel Tower, for the couple of days before the show. I was trying to enjoy taking the time off, especially out of the UK, with my family. It couldn't have been better, I suppose, really.

★*★

I'd never done a live gig outside of a studio without Leo. Lovely Leo had always been a part of it, of everything I was doing.

Adam Bede was very nice to me. Charming, in fact. He came to see me before the show to ask how I was, and did I mind, next time he was in the UK, if he contacted me. 'Perhaps we could, you know, go to a nice restaurant?'

Ben had come through with a picture message just before Adam had knocked on my dressing room door. Ben's face appeared on my mobile, as if he'd had a premonition of

Adam's arrival. 'DON'T ERASE ME', his text said.

'Don't erase me.' Almost as if I could, in reality, have taken him from my memory, blotting him out altogether.

Then my memory went. Not mine, my telephone memory. The battery died. But I could remember it all, all of it. Nothing was gone from me. I still wanted my friends. I loved them. I loved people.

'Would that be all right?' Adam Bede said. 'If I come and see you?'

I thought about it. The memory on my mobile had gone with the battery; but my own memory remained intact.

Don't erase me!

A week had gone by without any contact with Beccs. I didn't try to speak to her, but she hadn't tried to get through to me, either. And she'd caused the problems, not me!

So a week passed and the time had come for the Eiffel Tower gig. I'd wanted Beccs to come with us to Paris. That, along with everything else, was falling through. All of it, everything we had trashed. Without a sound.

I couldn't stand it. It shouldn't have to end like this. Not like this! Just – not like this!

It must have been nearly time for me to go on. The Eiffel Tower looked fabulous at night, lit up, with the huge stage at one end of the park, the sea of illuminated faces like the real heart of central Paris. I felt nervous, unprepared, as if I'd never held a crowd before, as if an audience this size was new to me, and frightening.

She was in; I'd made sure by watching her come home from school. My heart was thumping as I went up to her front door. It took all my courage and resolve to ring, to knock, to ring again. She didn't answer.

I took out my mobile and punched out a text. My finger shook over the 'send' button:

'I KNOW YOU'RE IN THERE!'

Someone called to me to come up to the off-stage wings where the next performers awaited entrance. The nag of my nervousness turned in my stomach, fluttering, but too fast and furious to be mere weak-winged butterflies. More like bats, in the dark. This, of all times, felt the hardest, the loneliest. I needed Leo now, right now, to settle me. I needed Beccs to be with me, as she had been always. I needed them, both of them. I didn't think I could do this any more, without them. I was just too scared to go on alone.

***

On Beccs's front doorstep, a week away from our last conversation, the staircase footfalls I waited for, the urgency of Beccs's unfailing friendship I needed, failed again. My ear to the dead letterbox told me she didn't want to face me. But all the while friends do not face one another when they should, is the longer and longer while of friendship's end. The eternity of a dear friendship's end occurred to me again as my ear was pressed against the shell of my friend's seemingly empty house. But that house was not empty, I knew, however silent it seemed.

Alone, the Eiffel Tower appeared too populated, too foreign and alien to me. I couldn't win over such a crowd, not on my own, not all on my own!

I dialled her mobile number. In the house, no phone chimed football-supporter tunes, nobody made moves to answer or acknowledge me. My signal dropped into an empty void, the shell of the house that registered no sign. My call went into voicemail, with Beccs saying:

'If you don't leave a message, I'll never call you back.'

Ben's old message, now recycled and put once again to good use. I didn't leave a message. Perhaps she'd never call me back.

The house phone, when I dialled the number, rang reverberating up the silent staircase. Wherever Beccs was in the house, she'd surely hear this, and it would be obvious who it was, immediately after the text message had been received. So I knew what it must have meant when she didn't come running downstairs or answer her phone or make a single move towards the ringing house phone or towards me, on her front doorstep.

I walked away from her. She let me go. Walking from the house, I glanced back. An upstairs curtain fell against my turned face, drawing a blind, drawing a terrible conclusion.

Thirty-One

Of all times, this felt the hardest and loneliest. That walk from dressing rooms to edge of stage felt so long alone, badly lit as it was, such an eye-strain to see far enough ahead to know where you were going. For what felt like a long, long time, I felt lost. I needed Leo.

'Oh, do come on, Lovely!' he suddenly flapped into view in front of me. 'What are you up to? Get a move on. Really . . . oh, my! That outfit! It's you! I can't say any more.'

Not ten seconds after the curtain falling, and the door crashed aside and Beccs ran out like a frantic goal-scorer. 'Don't go!' she cried. She had a pair of little earphones dangling round her neck.

'Amy! Don't go!' She held up a hand in a halting motion, which stopped me.

We both stopped.

Beccs. Oh, my friend.

Her face, looking into mine, was searching for the right thing to say. She couldn't find it. And she tried so hard, a tear fell from the corner of her eye.

'Where are you going?' she said, which wasn't the right thing, but was better than nothing.

Standing there, I thought I'd be wondering where I stood

in our relationship; but we stood, face to face, a tear falling from Beccs to the ground between us.

'Don't go,' she said. 'Amy, don't go.'

All the things I thought I might say to her, all the opening statements I'd rehearsed evaporated, leaving me grounded, floundering after how I now felt about what she'd done.

'What have I done?' she said.

I shook my head. Words, if they were there at all, couldn't have got past my constricted throat. I had to struggle hard to swallow.

'Oh, Amy, what have I done?'

She looked down. Tears plopped onto the garden path.

She looked up. 'I've been so ill,' she said. 'How can you ever – how can you ever –'

'Beccs,' I said, releasing my throat.

'Beccs,' and I reached out for her.

'It's simply you!' Leo said, twirling and blossoming with excitement. 'I can't say any more.'

He could, you know Leo. You and I know Leo, and I'm so glad. The desperation and loneliness just lifts away when Leo's like he is, being Leo, and lovely, which is all that can be said.

'Every inch the star!' he shimmered, like another little star, but a real one, very high up. 'How do you feel, my Sweet?'

'How can you ever forgive me?'

I had said I wasn't crying any more. I'd done with crying.

I'd lied. Now I cried, because Beccs did, like I'd never seen before.

'How can you ever forgive me?'

We cried. I forgave her.

'I told them,' she cried. 'I told them. I told them.' She hiccough-cried, wetting almost her whole face. She looked so desperate, so sweet and lovely I felt like Leo, ready to forgive the world. Certainly, I was prepared to forgive Beccs anything, anything!

'No,' I said. I was shaking, my own tears falling like my friend's. She wiped my face with her fingers. 'No you never. You told *him*.'

'That's the same thing!'

'No, it's not. You trusted James. He betrayed your trust.'

'I betrayed yours.'

'That's what I thought, at first. But you didn't, Beccs. I'm not having that. You put your trust in him. He sold it on to Barry Bone.'

'They paid him!' she said, despairing. 'He sold us out, for money. To be big, with his mates. They knew. That's how I knew. He boasted, he couldn't help it. Someone told me, but I already suspected it.'

'When you saw the headline about my trashing Jag's mobile?'

She nodded. A sheet of tears drew a blind down over her face. 'I think I knew. I hate him for what he's done to us.'

'Beccs,' I said, looking very seriously into her face, 'listen to me. He's done nothing to us, do you hear me? Nobody can do anything to us, ever! It doesn't matter what they try, it won't work. Nobody can touch us Beccs,' I said, as she hugged me. 'We're too special.'

'We are,' she sobbed. 'We're too special. Too special.'

'Don't forget it,' I said.

'I'll never forget it,' she said.

'They can't break us, Beccs. Ever.'

'Never,' she said.

Never, ever.

'How do you feel, my Sweet?'

'Leo, I feel lovely.'

'You are!'

'I feel like – love. I can still give, Leo. And I'm not going to stop giving, because that's how I am. I am who I am. I can't stop giving.'

'Then we'll just have to take better care of each other,' he said.

'So you can't ever go away from me,' I said.

He flapped. 'Go away? Whatever makes you think I'll ever want to go away?'

I loved Leo. 'Leo I – '

'Enough, Lovely! You're on in a minute. Be ready. Are you ready?'

'Yes, I'm ready. I'm ready for anything.'

'Then break a leg, Sweet. But just don't break a leg.'

No big explosive entry this time. I was not the biggest star of this show. In France, I still took my turn, walking out onto the stage like a newcomer, taking my position with my little head-mike clipped on as the band started up with the intro to Adam Bede's slow song, *Never Let You Go*:

I think I see you everywhere,
Same face, same smile, same eyes, same hair,
You are exactly as you were before.
For me, time has no power,
At least now over you any more.

For Geoff? Yes. But also for Ben.

For me, time has no power,
At least now over you any more.
You'll never regret another day, another hour,
I'll never erase you.
I'll never let you go.

And for Beccs and me: because there she was, at the side of the stage, my biggest fan and my best friend.

I'll never let you go.

At the end of the song the audience went wild as Adam stepped onto the stage with me. He was nice, very good looking. Charming. We sang together:

Walking round in a haze
Talking like a lunatic
Through restless nights and dog-tired days
Love's making me feel sick.

But I'd rather feel
So very ill
Than never be in love at all.

Yes, I'd rather feel
So very ill
Than never be in love at all.

Love makes me sick
But I can't take a pill
Love makes me sick
I must like being ill
Love makes me sick
And it gives me such a thrill

Love Makes Me Sick, although it didn't, because I had more love in me than I could ever want or need, and I felt fine.

'Yes,' I had said to Adam, earlier, 'yes, please come and see me when you're next in the UK. Come and see me,' because Ben was just a friend. I'd never erase him from my memory, because he was a special friend. But Adam was – well, as he squeezed my hand at the end of our song, as he turned smiling at me as the audience applauded – well Adam was – charming. And I was charmed.

***Thirty-Two**

'The art of recording,' Ben was saying, 'Is the art of gentle compression.'

We were back in the same exclusive restaurant, Beccs and Ben and I, the one we'd been to the last time we three had been out together. Ben wasn't drinking beer this time. He wasn't smoking either.

'He's so different,' I said to Beccs, when Ben had gone to the loo.

'Yeah,' she said. 'So is James Benton, since I gave him that slap.'

'Is he?' I said.

'Yeah. He knows now to stay away from me, or he'll get another one.'

I had to laugh.

'Somebody should have given him a good smack ages ago,' she said. 'To sort his head out.'

'It can't be that easy. Otherwise I'd just slap everyone and sort everything every time.'

'Perhaps you should,' Beccs said, 'including me.'

So I reached out and made to slap her, but touched her cheek. 'That'll do for you,' I said. 'That's you sorted.'

She and Ben had brought me here because, they said, they had a surprise for me. I was expecting some kind of gift. Last time we were here together I'd given them both new picture-messaging mobile phones. This time they had given me nothing so far, no clues as to what the nature of their surprise might be. We had a pleasant meal together, with all three of us comfortable with these surroundings and in each other's company. Beccs and I were still not as we would have been without Ben, but then it was never the same if anybody else was with us. When we were alone together we were like a single unit, two halves of the same thing. In the last few days, Beccs and I had been closer than ever. We'd spent the whole weekend together, talking, laughing, crying. Laughing, mainly. It's funny, when you laugh that much, how easy it is to cry. Then, crying, how easy to burst out laughing again. Honestly, the laughing and crying we did, I sometimes thought we were never coming out of it again. We didn't, in actual fact, not unchanged, anyway.

But there we were, finally, with Ben in the expensive West End restaurant having a nice time. And there I was, wondering what the surprise was they had for me. There was no sign of anything at all, no wrapped present, no conspiratorial glances between Beccs and Ben.

'The art of recording,' Ben was saying, 'is the art of gentle compression.'

'What does that mean?' Beccs said.

'It doesn't matter what it means,' I said. 'Isn't it beautiful?'

'It means,' Ben said, 'that I've got an awful lot to learn. It means,' he said, looking at me now, 'that I'm looking forward to learning the art of gentle compression, and I'm looking forward to all the things I'm going to achieve in the future.'

I glanced at Beccs. She smiled.

'No,' Ben said, 'it really means – thanks, Amy, for helping me sort my head out.'

'Oh,' Beccs said, to make us laugh, 'a good old slap would have done that for you.' And she pretended to slap him in the way I had pretended to her.

So I reached out and slapped him too, in friendship. 'So what's this surprise you've got for me?' I asked them both. 'I'm dying to find out. What is it?'

They looked at each other in a conspiratorial way for the first time. 'Shall we tell her?' Beccs said.

Ben thought about it. 'Nah,' he said. 'Let's go.'

'Go?' I said.

'Come on,' Beccs said. 'Let's go.'

'Where?' I said.

But they were up, with the waiters buzzing with jackets and farewells and we were on the street walking the way Ben and I had walked the last time we'd left that restaurant together.

'But where are we going?'

But nothing; nothing but their knowing grins and our hurrying footsteps along the London pavements. I suppose the Underground thundered underground, but I was aware of no metallic grind, no frantic traffic threat as we made our way to – to wherever we were on our way to.

Leicester Square? Like last time with Ben, we made our way there, turning the corner where the elaborate Swiss bells were chiming to see the surprise my closest friends and so many others had prepared for me.

The square had been closed off. But we were escorted through the cordon of crowd crash-barriers to where the eight guys drummed, exactly as before, and the girls danced and the solo guitarist picked out other people's tunes. The whole thing was exactly as before, but crowd controlled and punctuated by 'cherry-pickers', a kind of thin crane with a camera and some sound equipment fitted.

'What is this?' I cried, swinging round to face my friends.

Beccs and Ben were laughing, but the drums were beating and the girls were dancing and a group of ballooned-up party girls were approaching me exactly as before. They pretended they didn't know who I was until Ben whipped my cap off and the girls screamed and Ben ran off to collect the guitarist, leading him along by his amp lead.

We were filming a video. This was an actual, unrehearsed video-shoot to be included in the footage for *Love Makes Me Sick*.

'We thought you'd prefer it this way!' Leo appeared and said, before blending into the crowd surrounding the drummers, the dancers and me.

He was right. I loved it like this. This was going to be good.

But I'd rather feel
So very ill
Than never be in love at all.
Yes, I'd rather feel
So very ill
Than never be in love at all!

Yes, I'd rather feel so very ill. Like this, I still had more love in me than I could ever want or need.

Love makes me sick
But I can't take a pill
Love makes me sick
I must like being ill
Love makes me sick
And it gives me such a thrill!

We loved it. I lived it.

One of the girls, the street dancers screamed with me, like I do, with me, like I do. 'It must be really great being you,' she shouted.

I hugged her. We danced.

Yes, it was true; it was really, really great being me, being Amy Peppercorn. It was really great, just being me. It was!

Also by John Brindley

Amy Peppercorn: Starry-Eyed And Screaming

Sixteen-year-old Amy Peppercorn has a lot to scream about. Her best friend Beccs is being lured away by that hateful boy beacon, Kirsty. School sucks. Her family are impossible to live with. Know the feeling?

Then – although she SO didn't mean to – she falls under the spell of the cool, irresistible Ben and joins his band. Everything changes.

Because Amy's scream is her fortune. She's going to be a pop sensation and she's on her way.

As John Brindley charts her road to fame there is glitz and excitement. But secrets and startling revelations also unfold in a story that packs a huge emotional punch.

Stardom has its price – how much will Amy pay?

Amy Peppercorn: Living The Dream

Amy *is* an overnight sensation. She *is* top of the pops.

Amy's living the dream – and she's carrying the guilt. Geoff is dead. Ben is on remand. She's lost best friend Beccs and even her Mum seems out of reach.

On tour, in the midst of glamour and fame, starry performances and screaming crowds, Amy's never been so utterly lonely.

Cue the mysterious Jag Mistri – he seems so perfect, a friend who can make the dream last forever.

Heady success and shocking deception walk hand-in-hand in John Brindley's heart-searching, revealing sequel to *Amy Peppercorn: Starry-eyed and Screaming*, about the joys and sorrows of being a teenage star.